"You Don't Know Me Well Enough To Know I Have An Ego."

"Please." She gave a short laugh. "Look at you. Of course you do."

"I think that was a compliment."

"See?" she said. "Ego."

"Touché. So, how are you going to help me with the bet?" She smiled, and he felt the powerful slam of it hit him like a sledgehammer.

"Why, First Sergeant Reilly, if some gorgeous woman shows up, I'll just throw myself on you like you were a live grenade."

Aidan looked up and down slowly, completely. Then he shook his head. "Terry Evans, with that kind of help, I'm a dead man...."

Dear Reader,

July is a month known for its heat and fireworks, as well as the perfect time to take that vacation. Well, why not take a break and enjoy some hot sparks with a Silhouette Desire? We've got six extraordinary romances to share with you this month, starting with *Betrayed Birthright* by Sheri WhiteFeather. This seventh title in our outstanding DYNASTIES: THE ASHTONS series is sure to reveal some unbelievable facts about this scandalous family.

USA TODAY bestselling author Maureen Child wraps up her fabulous THREE-WAY WAGER series with *The Last Reilly Standing*. Or is he getting down on bended knee? And while some series are coming to a close, new ones are just beginning, such as our latest installment of the TEXAS CATTLEMAN'S CLUB: THE SECRET DIARY. Cindy Gerard kicks off this six-book continuity with *Black-Tie Seduction*. Also starting this month is Bronwyn Jameson's PRINCES OF THE OUTBACK. These Australian hunks really need to be tamed, beginning with *The Rugged Loner*.

A desert beauty in love with a tempting beast. That's the theme of Nalini Singh's newest release, *Craving Beauty*—a story not to be missed. And the need to break a long-standing family curse leads to an attraction that's just *Like Lightning*, an outstanding romance by Charlene Sands.

Here's hoping you enjoy all the fireworks Silhouette Desire has to offer you…this month and all year long!

Best,

Melissa Jeglinski

Melissa Jeglinski
Senior Editor
Silhouette Desire

Please address questions and book requests to:
Silhouette Reader Service
U.S.: 3010 Walden Ave., P.O. Box 1325, Buffalo, NY 14269
Canadian: P.O. Box 609, Fort Erie, Ont. L2A 5X3

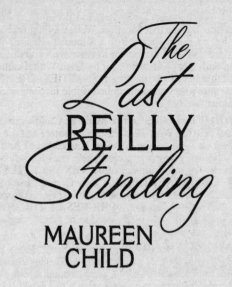

The Last
REILLY
Standing

MAUREEN CHILD

Published by Silhouette Books

America's Publisher of Contemporary Romance

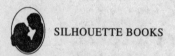 SILHOUETTE BOOKS

ISBN 0-373-76664-5

THE LAST REILLY STANDING

Copyright © 2005 by Maureen Child

All rights reserved. Except for use in any review, the reproduction
or utilization of this work in whole or in part in any form by any
electronic, mechanical or other means, now known or hereafter
invented, including xerography, photocopying and recording, or in
any information storage or retrieval system, is forbidden without
the written permission of the editorial office, Silhouette Books,
233 Broadway, New York, NY 10279 U.S.A.

All characters in this book have no existence outside the imagination of
the author and have no relation whatsoever to anyone bearing the same
name or names. They are not even distantly inspired by any individual
known or unknown to the author, and all incidents are pure invention.

This edition published by arrangement with Harlequin Books S.A.

® and TM are trademarks of Harlequin Books S.A., used under license.
Trademarks indicated with ® are registered in the United States Patent
and Trademark Office, the Canadian Trade Marks Office and in other
countries.

Visit Silhouette Books at www.eHarlequin.com

Printed in U.S.A.

Books by Maureen Child

Silhouette Desire

Have Bride, Need Groom #1059
The Surprise Christmas Bride #1112
Maternity Bride #1138
The Littlest Marine #1167
*The Non-Commissioned
  Baby* #1174
*The Oldest Living Married
  Virgin* #1180
Colonel Daddy #1211
Mom in Waiting #1234
Marine under the Mistletoe #1258
The Daddy Salute #1275
The Last Santini Virgin #1312
The Next Santini Bride #1317
Marooned with a Marine #1325

*Prince Charming in
  Dress Blues* #1366
His Baby! #1377
Last Virgin in California #1398
Did You Say Twins?! #1408
The SEAL's Surrender #1431
The Marine & the Debutante #1443
The Royal Treatment #1468
Kiss Me, Cowboy! #1490
Beauty & the Blue Angel #1514
Sleeping with the Boss #1534
Man Beneath the Uniform #1561
Lost in Sensation #1611
Society-Page Seduction #1639
†*The Tempting Mrs. Reilly* #1652
†*Whatever Reilly Wants...* #1658
†*The Last Reilly Standing* #1664

Silhouette Special Edition

Forever...Again #1604

Harlequin Historicals

Shotgun Grooms #575
"Jackson's Mail-Order Bride"

Silhouette Books

Love Is Murder
"In Too Deep"

Dynasties: Summer in Savannah
"With a Twist"

*Bachelor Battalion
†Three-Way Wager

MAUREEN CHILD

is a California native who loves to travel. Every chance they get, she and her husband are taking off on another research trip. The author of more than sixty books, Maureen loves a happy ending and still swears that she has the best job in the world. She lives in Southern California with her husband, two children and a golden retriever with delusions of grandeur.

Visit her Web site at www.maureenchild.com.

One

One

Aidan Reilly was so close to winning, he could almost taste the celebratory champagne. Okay, beer.

The longest three months of his *life* were coming to an end. Only three more weeks to go and he'd be the winner of the bet he and his brothers had entered into so grudgingly at the beginning of the summer.

He shuddered thinking about it, even now. Ninety days of no sex and the winner received the whole ten thousand dollars left to the Reilly triplets by their great-uncle. It was all their older brother, Father Liam Reilly's fault. He'd waved the red flag of challenge at them, insisting that priests were *way* tougher than Marines—since he'd had to give up sex for *life*. Well, no self-respecting Reilly ever turned down a challenge. Though this one had been tougher to survive than any of them had thought.

Brian and Connor had already folded—which left Aidan alone to hold up the family honor—and make sure their older brother, Father Liam, couldn't laugh his ass off at all of them.

It wasn't even about the money anymore, Aidan thought, staring across their table at the Lighthouse restaurant at Liam. Their older brother wanted them all to lose the bet so *he* could use the money for a new roof on his church. Well, Aidan wasn't about to tell him yet, but once he won this bet and had all of his brothers admitting that *he* was the strongest of the bunch then he planned on giving the money to Liam anyway.

He didn't need it. Being a single Marine, he made enough money to support himself and that was all he cared about. He'd never entered the bet for the *money*.

What he wanted was to *win*.

He leaned back on the bench seat and avoided letting his gaze drift around the crowded restaurant. The Lighthouse was a spot favored by families, so he was pretty safe. The only women he had to worry about in here were the waitresses—and they looked too damn good for his well-being. And at that thought, he shifted his gaze back to the surface of his drink.

"Worried?" Brian muttered, lifting his glass to take a sip of beer.

"Hell no—I'm closing in on the finish line."

"Yeah, well. You haven't won yet."

"Only a matter of time." Aidan smiled, while keeping his gaze fixed on his glass of beer.

"Gotta say," Connor admitted, leaning forward to brace his forearms on the table. "I'm impressed. Didn't think you'd last this long."

"I did," Liam said, taking a drink of his own beer.

"Yeah?" Aidan lifted his gaze and grinned at his older brother, ignoring the other two—identical replicas of himself. "Because I'm the strongest, right?" he spared a quick look at his fellow triplets and sneered. "Hah."

"Actually," Liam said smiling, "it's because you've always been the most stubborn."

Beside him, Connor laughed and Aidan gave him a quick elbow jab. "I'll take what I can get," he said.

"You've still got three weeks to go," Brian reminded him from his seat beside Liam. "And while Connor and I are getting regular sex from our lovely wives, you're a man *alone*."

There was that. Aidan scowled as he took a sip of his beer and made a point of keeping his gaze locked on the three men sitting with him. One glimpse of some gorgeous blonde or a curvy redhead or God help him, a pretty brunette and he'd have to go home and take yet another cold shower. Hell, he'd spent so much time in icy water lately between the showers and his work as a USMC rescue diver, he felt like a damn penguin.

"I can make it," he said tightly.

"Three weeks is a long time," Connor pointed out.

"I've already made it through *nine* weeks," Aidan reminded them. Nine long, miserable weeks. But the worst was over now. He was on the downhill slide. He'd make it. Damned if he wouldn't.

"Yeah," Liam said with a knowing smile, "but everyone knows the *last* mile of the race is always the most difficult."

"Thanks a lot."

"Twenty-one whole days," Liam said, making the three weeks sound even longer.

"How many *hours* is that?" Brian wondered.

"Man, you guys are cruel."

"What're brothers for?" Connor asked.

Aidan shook his head and kicked back on the bench seat. Ignoring Liam and smirking at his identical brothers, he said, "Do I have to remind you two what wusses you both were? How you both caved so easily?"

Brian grimaced and Connor shifted in his seat.

"Nope," Aidan muttered, smiling to himself, "guess not."

Bright and early the next morning, Terry Evans took a long look around the Frog House bookstore and told herself this would be a snap. A good change of pace. An interesting bump in the long, straight highway of her life.

Then a five-year-old boy grabbed a book away from a three-year-old girl, resulting in a howl rarely heard outside of the nature channel on TV during a documentary on coyotes.

Terry winced and smiled at the harried moms as they raced to snatch up their respective children. Oh, yeah, she thought, suddenly rethinking her generous offer to help out a friend. A snap.

There were kids all over the bookstore. No big surprise there, since the shop catered to those ten and under. Not to mention their moms.

Frog House was filled with pillow-stuffed nooks and crannies, where kids could curl up with a book while their mothers sat at the small round tables, sipping fresh coffee. The kids had a great time, exploring a place where everything was "hands on" and the moms could relax, knowing that their children couldn't possibly get into trouble here.

Donna had wanted a kid-friendly store and she'd built a child's fantasy. Murals of fairy tales covered the walls, and bookshelves were low enough that even the top shelf was within reach of tiny hands. There was a coloring corner, with child-size tables littered with coloring books and every color crayon imaginable. During story hour, every day at four o'clock, at least twenty kids sat on the bright rugs, listening with rapt attention to the designated reader.

Terry sighed a little and smiled as the squabbling kids settled down again, each with their own book this time. If her gaze lingered on the five-year-old boy a moment or two longer, she told herself no one but she would notice.

Her heart ached, but it was an old pain now, more familiar than startling. She'd learned to live with it. Learned that it would never really go away.

And if truth were told, she didn't want to lose that pain. Because if she did, she would have to lose the memories that caused it and she would never allow herself to do *that*.

"Excuse me?"

She turned her gaze from the kids at the "play time" table that was littered with discarded coloring books and half-eaten crayons, to face... *A MAN*.

At first sight of him, she immediately thought of him in Capital Letters. As her temperature climbed, she took a second or two to check him out completely. Tall, easily over six feet, he wore a black T-shirt with USMC stamped on the left side of his impressive chest.

Not surprising to find a Marine standing in the shop. After all, Baywater, South Carolina, was just a short drive down the road from Parris Island, the Marine Corps Recruit Depot—not to mention the Marine Corps Air Station in Beaufort.

But *this* Marine had her complete attention.

The Man's muscles rippled beneath the soft, worn fabric of his shirt and when he folded his arms across his chest, she nearly applauded the move. His waist was narrow, hips nonexistent and his long legs were hugged by worn, threadbare jeans. The hem of those jeans stacked up on the top of his battered cowboy boots.

Oh, my.

She lifted her gaze to his face and felt her internal temperature spike another ten points. Black hair, unfortunately militarily short, ice-blue eyes, a squared off jaw and a straight nose that could have come off a Roman coin. Then he smiled and she saw gorgeous white teeth and a dimple, God help her, in his right cheek.

Did it suddenly get hot in there?

"Hello?" He lifted one hand and snapped his fingers in front of her face. "You okay?"

Minor meltdown, she wanted to say, but for a change, Terry wisely kept her mouth shut. For a second. "Sorry. What can I do for you?"

He gave her a slow smile that notched up the heat in her southern regions and she groaned inwardly. She'd walked into that one. Figured he was a man who could take a simple statement and make it sound like an invitation to sweaty sheets.

"Can I help you?" She shook her head. This wasn't getting any better.

Finally, though, he quit smiling, stepped up closer to her and looked around the bookstore as if searching for something in particular. "Can you tell me where Donna Fletcher is?" he asked, shifting his gaze back to hers.

Terry checked her wristwatch, then looked up at him again. "Right now, she's about halfway to Hawaii."

"Already?" He looked stunned. "She didn't tell me she was leaving early."

One of Terry's perfectly arched, dark blond eyebrows lifted. "Was there some special reason she *should?*"

He scraped one hand across his square jaw. "Suppose not," he admitted, then blew out a breath. "It's just that I'm supposed to be doing a project for her and—"

Realization dawned. Actually, Terry felt as if she were in a cartoon and someone had just penciled in a lightbulb over her head. "You're Aidan Reilly."

His gaze snapped to hers. "How'd you know that?"

She smiled, shook her hair back and told herself that she was going to have to have a long conversation with Donna one of these days.

Her very best friend had told her all about the bet that Aidan had entered into with his brothers—and that she, Donna, had offered Aidan the bookstore as a safe place to hide out from women. In exchange, of course, for Aidan agreeing to build a "reading castle" for the kids. But, she'd never mentioned that Aidan Reilly looked like a walking billboard for good sex.

Actually, *exceptional* sex.

Maybe even *amazing, incredible, earthshaking* sex.

Terry was beginning to suspect a setup.

Donna, a romantic at heart, had decided that what

Terry needed was a permanent man. Someone to love. Someone to love *her*. The fact that Terry wasn't interested in anything more permanent than a long weekend, didn't really enter into Donna's plans.

Aidan Reilly, it seemed, was the latest salvo fired in an ongoing battle.

And though Terry still wasn't interested, she had to admit that Donna was using some first-class ammunition.

He was snapping his fingers in her face again. She reached up and swatted his hand away. "You keep doing that. It's annoying."

"You keep zoning out," he said. "Even more annoying."

Good point. "Sorry. I'm a little tired. Got in late last night and had to open the shop first thing this morning."

"Fascinating," Aidan replied. "Still doesn't tell me how you know my name and why Donna didn't tell me she was leaving three days early."

"Donna told me your name, and by the way, I'm Terry Evans," she said and smiled at a woman who walked up and handed her a book ready for purchase. Walking around behind the counter, Terry rang up the sale, bagged the book and handled the credit card transaction. When she'd finished, she wished the woman a good day, turned back to face Mr. Tall, Dark and Gorgeous and picked up right where she left off. "And I'm guessing she didn't tell you she was leaving early because she didn't think it was any of your business."

He scowled at her and strangely enough, she found *that* expression even more intriguing than the flash of dimple when he smiled.

"I told her I'd take her and the kids to the airport," he muttered. "But she wasn't supposed to leave until Friday."

"She got an earlier flight and grabbed it," Terry explained with a shrug. "I took her and the kids to the airport," she added, remembering the warm little hugs and the sticky kisses she'd received last night as the Fletcher family set off for their vacation.

He blew out a breath. "Probably good. She could use the break."

"Yes," Terry said. "She really can. Her folks live on Maui, you know and they're dying to see the kids and with—"

"—Tony deployed overseas," Aidan finished for her, "she needed to get away."

"Yeah. Worry takes a lot out of you." Heck, Terry wasn't even married to Tony Fletcher and she worried about his safety. She couldn't imagine what it was like for a Marine wife. Having to run the house, keep sane, deal with kids, all while keeping one corner of your brain saying a constant stream of prayers for your husband.

"So I'm told."

"But," Terry said, waggling her index finger in a

"follow me" signal, "Donna told me all about your 'problem' before she left."

"Is that right?"

She nodded as she stepped behind the glass case containing fresh muffins, brownies and cookies. Grabbing a tall paper cup from the stack near the espresso machine, she added, "And she told me how you like your coffee."

He smiled again, and Terry told herself to ignore the wildly fluctuating heat barometer inside her. Seriously, though, the man was like a lightning rod. He channeled hormones and turned them into heat that simmered just under a woman's skin. Pretty potent stuff.

"The day's looking a little better already."

She smiled, glanced at him, then looked away quickly—watching Aidan Reilly was *not* conducive to concentration. And running the complicated machine with dials and steamers and nozzles and whatchamacallits required concentration. While the steamer hissed, she risked another quick glance at him and noted that he was now leaning on the glass countertop, watching her closely.

His eyes were blue enough to swim in, she thought idly and wondered just how many women had taken that particular plunge.

"So what did Donna say, exactly?" he asked.

Clearing her throat noisily, she said, "She told me about the silly bet you and your brothers made."

"Silly?"

"Completely." She pulled the stainless steel pitcher of frothing milk free of the heating bars, then wiped them down with a damp towel. As she poured the hot milk into the cup, she kept talking. "She told me that she'd offered you the use of the bookstore as a sort of demilitarized zone and in return, you're going to build a castle for the kids."

That was how Donna had put it, anyway. She remembered the brief explanation she'd gotten only the night before.

Aidan's a sweetie, Donna told her, packing up the last of the kids' stuff. *But he's determined to win this stupid bet. So I told him he could hang out at the bookstore when he's off base. It's pretty safe there since not many single women come to the shop. And in return, he's promised to build a "reading castle" for my littlest customers.*

And I'm supposed to protect him from women? Terry asked.

Please, honey, Donna said laughing. *He doesn't need protecting. He just needs a safe zone to wait out the rest of the bet.*

And you're being so accommodating, why?

Donna closed the suitcase, then spotted a ragged blanket with more holes than fabric, sighed and opened the suitcase again to stuff Mr. Blankie inside. When she was finished, she sat on the bed and looked up at Terry. Because he's been a good friend while Tony's been deployed. He comes over here if I need the sink fixed or if the car takes a dump. He and Tony went through boot camp together. They're like best friends and Aidan's...family.

Which was why, Terry told herself, she was standing here staring into a pair of blue eyes that shone with all kinds of exciting sparks.

"Demilitarized zone, huh?" he asked. "Well, that's one way of putting it."

She smiled and spooned on a layer of foam before snapping a plastic lid on the coffee cup and handing it over. "Donna says you spend your time off from the base here, hiding out because most of her customers are young married moms—and therefore *safe*."

He took a sip of coffee, lifted both eyebrows and nodded. "Not bad."

"Thank you."

"And I don't consider it hiding out."

"Really? What do you call it?"

"Strategic maneuvering."

Terry smiled. "Whatever helps. So, you've got to last three more weeks without sex to win the bet."

"That's about the size of it."

Now it was her turn to lift her brows and smile at him.

Took Aidan a minute, to catch the joke playing out in her eyes, but finally he grinned in appreciation. Not only was she gorgeous, but she had a quick, wicked mind. Normally he liked that in a woman.

But this wasn't "normal." This was a time when

he had to stay stronger than he ever had before. And having Terry around for the next few weeks wasn't going to make life easier.

She was still watching him, a playful smirk on her mouth. "This isn't about size."

"It's *always* about size," she retorted and stepped out from behind the espresso machine. "This time, it's just about the size of your ego."

He followed her as she walked to the kids play table and idly straightened up the mess. He tried not to notice the fall of her pale blond hair against her porcelain cheek. Just like he tried to ignore the curve of her hip or the way the hem of her skirt lifted in back as she bent over the scattered books. And he *really* tried not to notice her legs.

What the hell had Donna been thinking? Bringing in Terry Evans to help him stay away from sex was like lighting a fire to prevent heat.

Oh, yeah.

This was gonna work out just fine.

Scowling slightly, he said, "You don't know me well enough to know I have an ego."

"Please." She gave a short laugh and looked at him over her shoulder. "Look at you. Of course you do."

"I think that was a compliment."

"See?" she pointed out. "Ego."

"Touché."

She gave him a brief, elegant nod.

He watched while she wiped up a crayon mess and

when she straightened and tossed her hair back from her face, he said, "So you're going to help me win the bet, huh?"

"You got it."

"How?"

She smiled and he felt the powerful slam of it hit him like a sledgehammer.

"Why, First Sergeant Reilly, if some gorgeous woman shows up, I'll just throw myself on you like you were a live grenade."

He looked her up and down slowly, completely. Then he shook his head. "Terry Evans…*that* kind of help and I'm a dead man."

Two

Summer in South Carolina could bring a grown man—even a *Marine*—to his knees weeping.

And September, though technically the beginning of fall, was actually summer's last chance to drum every citizen of the South into the dirt. Today, summer was doing a hell of a job of it.

Aidan paused, tipped his head back and stared up at the sweeping expanse of blue sky, looking for a cloud. *Any* cloud. But there was nothing to blot the heat of the sun and no shade nearby in the alley behind the bookstore.

He could have worked inside, but being out in the heat, away from Terry Evans made him feel just a little *safer*. Not that he was generally a man who ran for cover. Actually he was just the opposite. He liked the thrill of a risk. The punch of adrenaline when it raced through him. The sensation of balancing on the fine edge between life and death.

And he was smart enough to know that it wasn't adrenaline he felt when he looked at Donna's friend Terry. It was heat, pure and simple. The kind of heat he had to avoid for three more long, agonizing weeks.

"Donna," he muttered, "what in the hell were you thinking?"

He got no answer, of course, so he focused instead on the pile of wooden planks in front of him. "Just do the job, idiot."

Aidan had learned early the importance of focusing on the task at hand, despite the distractions around him. In the Corps, that focus could mean the difference between life and death.

And God knew, Terry Evans was a distraction.

The woman's laugh rang out a little too often. And her voice, when she spoke to the kids streaming in and out of the specialty bookstore, was soft and dreamy. Just the kind of voice a man liked to hear coming from the pillow beside his.

"Yeah. Concentrating." Aidan muttered the words as he slammed a hammer down onto a nail head. The solid slam against the wood jolted up his arm and hopefully, would shake thoughts of Terry out of his mind.

He couldn't believe his miserable luck. He'd

thought riding out the last three weeks of this bet would be easy, as long as he was here, in the bookstore. Actually he'd thought for sure that Donna would be closing the place while she was gone. Giving him a peaceful place to work and keep his head down until the bet was over.

But, no. Instead of peace and quiet, he got a Dolly Parton lookalike. Good thing he preferred brunettes—or he'd be a dead man already.

"How's it going?"

Her voice, from too close by, startled him, and Aidan slammed the hammer down onto his thumb. Pain streaked through him and stars danced in front of his closed eyes as he grabbed his injured thumb and squeezed. He clenched his jaw, trapping every cuss word he'd ever learned—and there were *many* of them—locked inside him.

Shifting a look at her, he nearly groaned again. Not from pain, this time. But from the absolute misery of having to look at a gorgeous woman and realize that he couldn't do what he'd normally do. Which was, offer to buy her a drink. Turn on the Reilly charm. Work his magic until he had her right where he wanted her.

In the dark.

In his bed.

Naked.

Oh, yeah, Aidan thought, his gaze locking on her sharp green eyes. The next three weeks were going to be a nightmare.

His thumb throbbed in time with the steady thud of his heart. While he stared at her, she cocked her hip, folded her arms beneath her truly impressive breasts and watched him with a benign look that told him she knew exactly what he'd been thinking.

"You know," she said finally, shaking her hair back from her face as a soft sea wind darted down the alley. "If you keep looking at women like that, you'll never last another three weeks."

He grinned and the pain in his thumb eased up a little. "Yeah? Irresistible, am I?"

She moved to the next step down from the porch, then sat down, her skirt hiking up, giving Aidan a better glimpse of her legs.

"Oh, I think I'll be able to restrain myself."

"Good to know."

"Besides," she pointed out, "you're not really interested in me."

"I'm not?" Intrigued, he forgot about his aching thumb. Hooking the claw tip of his hammer through a belt loop on his jeans, he planted one hand on the back wall of the bookstore, crossed one foot over the other and looked down at her.

"Nope." She smoothed her palms over her dark green skirt and demurely slid both legs to the side, crossing her feet neatly at the ankles.

A *demure* Dolly Parton.

Great.

"Face it, Aidan—I can call you Aidan, right?"

"That's my name."

"Well, face it, Aidan, you're a starving man and I'm a hamburger."

He snorted, looked her up and down thoroughly, then lifted his gaze back to hers. "Darlin', you're no hamburger. You're a steak."

She smiled. "Well, thanks. But like I said, you're a starving man. A man like you? No sex for nine weeks?" She shook her head slowly, still smiling. "I'm thinking that even hamburger would start looking like filet mignon."

"You have looked into a mirror lately, right?"

"Every day."

"And you see hamburger."

"I see eyes that are too big, a mouth that's too wide, a nose that turns up at the end, a scar on my eyebrow and a chin that has a stupid dent in it."

Amazing, Aidan thought. He'd been with enough women to know when one of them was fishing for compliments. And to be honest, most of them never had to fish around him. He was always the first to compliment a woman on her hair, her shoes, her smile…but this woman wasn't fishing.

"You know what I see?" He pushed away from the wall, hooked his thumbs into the back pockets of his jeans and looked down at her with a critical eye.

"Steak?"

"Grass-green eyes, a wide, luscious mouth, a pixie nose, an intriguing little blip in a perfectly curved eyebrow and a lickable dimple in a softly rounded chin."

She tipped her head to one side, studied him for a long moment, then blew out a breath. "Oh, you're very good."

"Yeah. And you're quite the filet yourself."

She held out one hand to him and Aidan took it. His fingers closed around hers and he could have sworn he felt the zing of something hot and lusty shoot straight from her fingertips to the area of his body most neglected lately.

When she was standing, Terry let go of his hand and rubbed her fingers together to dissipate the lingering heat she felt on her skin. "You know, it's a wonder you've lasted nine weeks," she said.

"Is that right?"

Forcing a laugh she didn't quite feel, she pointed out, "Hello? You just made a move on the woman who's supposed to be helping you *win* the stupid bet."

He scowled a bit.

"Seriously. You just can't help yourself, can you?"

"Excuse me?"

"Flirting." She absently brushed off the seat of her skirt with both hands, then stepped up onto the porch again. Grabbing hold of the doorknob, she gave it a twist, then turned to look at Aidan Reilly again. "Flirting is like breathing to you. You do it without even thinking about it."

"I wasn't flirting," he argued, grabbing the hammer off his belt loop.

"Please. 'Grass-green eyes? Lickable dimple?'"

"I was just—"

"Making a move," she finished for him and shook her head slowly. "And really? It was *so* blatant. Not subtle at all."

"Is that right?"

"Oh, yeah," Terry said and opened the door. "Does that kind of thing usually work for you? I mean, are women really that gullible? That easy to maneuver?"

He frowned up at her and Terry smiled inwardly. The man had more than enough confidence. She hadn't shattered him any. Maybe a couple of dings in a healthy ego, but she was pretty sure he could take it. Besides, if he ever found out how his words had hit her—about the fires still licking at her insides—well, let's just say, he wouldn't be winning any bets.

And Terry wasn't here for the scenery.

She wasn't here to get lucky with a Marine, either.

She was here to help out her dearest friend.

Then she'd be going back home.

"I don't 'maneuver' women," he said tightly.

"Sure you do," Terry quipped. "You just don't usually get caught doing it."

"You're not an easy woman, are you?"

"Depends on what you mean by *easy*."

"Not what you think I mean," he countered.

"I guess we'll see, won't we? In the next few weeks, that is."

He inhaled sharply, deeply and his scowl went just a little darker. "Exactly why did you come out here, anyway? Just to get a few digs in?"

"Actually," she said, pushing the door open, "I came to see if you wanted some iced tea."

"Oh." He balanced the hammer in one palm and slapped it rhythmically against his hand. "Well then, that'd be great. Thanks."

"It's in the fridge. Help yourself whenever you want it." She took a step inside, then stopped when he spoke up again.

"You're not going to bring it out here?"

Shaking her head again, Terry smiled. "Apparently you're used to women who fetch and carry. Sorry to disappoint you."

He gave her a slow smile. "I'll let you know when I'm disappointed, darlin'."

Terry sucked in a gulp of air, squared her shoulders and stepped into the air-conditioned haven of the small kitchen at the back of the store. She closed the door behind her, leaned against it and stared up at the ceiling. "Damn it, Donna. What have you gotten me into?"

The next couple of days were...*interesting*. If Terry could have looked at them objectively, she might have considered them an excellent exercise in self-control.

Instead she was just a little on edge and wondering how she was going to get through the next three weeks. Not only was Aidan Reilly an incredibly sexy man, but he was also a sexually starved man. As for Terry…she couldn't remember her last orgasm.

She'd done her share of dating—God, she hated that word—in the last few years. But being willing to go to dinner and a play with a man was a far cry from wanting him in her bed. She was picky, and she was the first to admit it. She didn't do one-night stands, and she couldn't bring herself to invest in a long-term relationship, so that pretty much left her out of the bedroom Olympics.

Which didn't really bother her most of the time. She kept busy. She was on more charitable boards than she could count, her fund-raising abilities were legendary and because of her gift with numbers, she'd been handed the reins of her family's financial empire three years ago.

This was the first "vacation" she'd had in years. Most people wouldn't consider working in a small-town bookstore a holiday. But for Terry, it was a treat.

Well, except for Aidan Reilly.

This whole situation just went to prove that Fate had a sense of humor. Putting a woman who'd been too long without sex in the position of keeping the world's sexiest man from *having* sex, had to be a cosmic joke.

Aidan cringed as he stepped into the blissfully

cool store and stopped in the open doorway leading from the kitchen to the main shop. Kids cried and shouted and laughed. Their mothers chitchatted, oblivious to the racket and he stood there, silently wishing he were out at sea.

He'd never really understood the draw of having children. To him, they looked like tiny anchors on long, heavy chains, designed to drag a man down. Besides, they were too damn loud.

He'd only come inside because he had the main structure of the reading castle finished and needed Terry to take a look at it. He laughed inwardly. Hell, he didn't really need her opinion. He'd gone over the plans and the basic idea with Donna, who'd already approved the whole thing.

What he really wanted was another look at the woman whose face had been invading his dreams for the last couple of nights. Self-preservation instincts told him to keep his distance—but the instinct that continuously prodded him to volunteer for dangerous missions was stronger. Which explained why he was now knee-deep in kids, waiting for a glimpse of Terry Evans.

Then there she was, moving through the sea of children like a sleek sailboat through choppy seas. Dipping and swaying with an instinctive elegance, she had a smile for each of the noisy kids and seemed completely unflustered by the racket.

She took a seat in a splash of afternoon sunlight,

as the children gathered on the floor in front of her. They quieted down slowly, giggles and grumbles fading into silence as Terry picked up a book and began to read. Her voice lifted and fell with the rhythm of the story, and Aidan, like the kids, couldn't take his gaze off her.

Terry held the colorful book up every now and then, to show the pictures and the kids laughed along with her as she acted out the different voices of the characters.

She was really something, Aidan thought. Even while a part of him really appreciated the picture she made—a larger part of him was shouting out *warning!*

If he had any sense he'd leave. He'd made it through nine long weeks of temptation and he wasn't about to lose the bet now, just because of a curvy blonde with hypnotic eyes.

He snorted. *"Hypnotic?"*

Man. He was in bad shape.

The kids laughed at something in the story and with an effort, he shook himself out of the stupor he'd slipped into. Screw having her check over his work. Screw hanging around this magnet for kiddies. He'd just go back outside, move the skeleton of the castle into the storage shed and get the hell outta Dodge.

He'd no sooner planned his escape than the cell phone he kept jammed in his jeans pocket let out a muffled ring. Digging for it, he checked the number, flipped the phone open and answered it while he headed for the back door.

"Get your butt back here, boy. We gotta move." J.T., the chopper pilot Aidan worked with, spoke fast. "Sport boat capsized about five miles out."

"On my way." Instantly, every thought but work raced out of his mind.

Aidan snapped the phone closed, jammed it into his pocket and headed out. He glanced back over his shoulder as he hit the doorway leading to the kitchen and the back door beyond. Terry's gaze slammed into his and he read a question in her eyes.

Just one more good reason to keep his distance, he told himself as he turned and stalked out. He wasn't a man who liked having to explain himself.

Having no one but himself to answer to kept life simple.

If he was lonely sometimes, that could be solved with friends or with a willing woman who knew not to expect any tomorrows out of him.

Terry Evans was not that kind of woman.

She had *tomorrows* written all over her.

Which should be enough to keep Aidan the hell away from her.

Three

The sea swallowed him.

In that one instant, when his head slipped below the cold water, Aidan wondered, as he always did, with just a small corner of his mind, if this might be the time the sea would keep him. Hold him, drag him down to the darkest water, where sunlight never touched. Where fish never swam. Where the cold was as deep as the darkness.

And just as quickly as it came, that thought disappeared, pushed aside so that he could do the job he'd trained for. He gave a couple of hard, powerful kicks, tipped his head back and breached the surface of the water. Cloud-dappled sunlight welcomed him, and he took a moment to find his bearings. Glancing to his left, he spotted the capsized sport boat about ten feet away, then shifted his gaze to the helicopter, hovering loudly about ten feet over head. The blades whipped the air, churning the already choppy water into a white foamed froth. The noise was tremendous. He lifted one arm, waved to Monk, hanging out the side of the chopper, then struck out swimming toward the boat and the two men perched on top of the upended hull.

"Man," the older one of the two shouted as he got nearer, "are we glad to see you guys."

Aidan grinned. Grabbing hold of the boat, he looked up at the men. They looked like father and son. The younger of the two couldn't have been more than seventeen. He looked scared and cold. Couldn't hardly blame him. Couldn't be easy to have your boat flip over on you.

He slapped the side of the boat. "You two need a ride?"

The helicopter came closer, dragging the orange steel cage basket through the water, skimming the surface, splashing through the whitecaps.

"Hell, yes," the older man shouted and slapped his son on the back. "Take Danny first."

Aidan shook his head as the basket came closer. Grabbing hold of it, he kept kicking, keeping his head above water and spitting out mouthfuls of it as it slapped him in the face. "No need. Basket's big enough. We all go."

The kid looked a little dubious and who could blame him? But to give him his due, he bit back on his own fears and slid down the side of the hull into the water. Aidan was ready for him, grabbing one arm with his free hand and tugging him closer. Over his radio, he heard Monk muttering.

"Move it along, will you, Reilly?"

"I'm getting there. Hold your horses."

"Who you talking to?" The kid shouted as he scrambled, with Aidan's help, into the basket and then inched to one side of it, with a two fisted, white knuckle grip on the rail.

"Them!" Aidan shouted and pointed skyward toward the hovering chopper. Then turning his gaze on the older man, he yelled, "Let's go!"

The man slid down and got into the basket with less trouble than his son had had. Then Aidan climbed in, and shouted, "Take us home, J.T."

While the chopper pilot moved off, the basket swung lazily into the air, like some amusement park ride. Monk operated the winch, raising the basket to the open door of the chopper, then when it was close enough, he grabbed hold and pulled it aboard.

"Everybody okay?" he shouted to be heard over the roar of the helicopter's engine.

"Fine." The older man climbed out, then reached

a hand to his son, to help him into the belly of the chopper. "Thanks for dropping by."

Monk draped the two guys in blankets while Aidan grinned and clambered out of the basket wiping water out of his face. "Always a pleasure," he yelled, feeling the adrenaline still pumping inside. "What happened to your boat?"

The man shook his head and leaned back against the shell of the chopper. "Damn thing started taking on water. Almost before we'd finished radioing for help, she got bottom heavy and did a roll, pitching us into the drink."

"Don't like boats," Monk shouted to no one in particular as he grabbed hold of one of the straps hanging from the roof of the chopper. "If God wanted us in the water, he would have given us gills."

Aidan laughed at his friend's solemn voice. The man hated water. Strange that he'd ended up in Search and Rescue. "But flying's okay?" he prodded, knowing the answer even before he asked the question.

"Hell, yes. It's *safer.* You ever see a tidal wave in the sky?"

While the man and his son relaxed to enjoy the ride, Aidan laughed at Monk and told himself he was a lucky man—jumping out of helicopters for a living—did it get any better than that?

By the next afternoon, Terry was ready for a break. She'd spent the last several days either in the bookstore, or tucked away in Donna's tiny, cottage-style house. She didn't know anyone in town—except for Aidan Reilly—and she hadn't seen him since he'd rushed out of the bookstore the previous afternoon.

Not that she *wanted* to see him, of course.

But spending too much time on her own only gave her too much time to think. Not necessarily a good thing.

Still, just because she was alone in a strange city, didn't mean she couldn't get out and mingle. Which was why she was spending her lunch hour walking along a crowded boardwalk, disinterestedly peering into the shop windows as she passed.

Although now, she was rethinking the whole, "get out and see some of Baywater" idea. The September sun beamed down from a brassy sky and simmered on the sidewalk before radiating back up to snarl at the pedestrians.

Even in a tank top and linen shorts, she felt the heat sizzling around her and realized that South Carolina muggy was *way* different than Manhattan muggy. She lifted her hair off her neck and let the soft ocean wind kiss her sweat dampened skin. One brief moment of coolness was her reward, but it was over almost before she could enjoy it.

All around her, families laughed and talked together. Kids with zinc oxide on their noses bounced in their tennies, eager to hit the beach. Young couples snuggled and held hands and the sound of cameras clicking was almost musical.

She came to the corner and stood on the sidewalk, watching the cars stream past along Main street. Well, "stream" was subjective. They were moving faster than she could walk, but traffic was pretty impressive for such a small town. When the light changed, she jumped off the curb and hurried across the street, unerringly headed for the dock and the ocean beyond. The nearer she got to the water, the brisker the wind felt and the ocean spray on her face was cool and welcome.

Boats lined the dock. Everything from small skiffs and dinky rowboats to huge pleasure crafts and mini yachts, bumped alongside each other like close friends at a cocktail party. Fishermen littered the pier, their poles and lines dangling over the weather beaten railings. A couple of skateboarders whizzed through the crowds, weaving in and out of the mob of people like dancers exhibiting precision steps. A balloon slipped free of a little girl's grasp and while her mother consoled her, the wind carried the bright splotch of red high into the sky.

Terry smiled to herself and kept walking. The scent of hot dogs and suntan lotion filled the air and as she passed a vendor, she stopped, giving in to hunger. She bought a hot dog and a soda, then carried them down a steep set of stairs to the rocks and the narrow beach below. Close enough to the pier that she heard the crowd, but far enough away that she felt just a touch of solitude.

Perching on a rock, she brought her knees up, took a bite of her hot dog and only half listened to the sounds around her as she focused her gaze on a couple of surfers, riding a low wave toward shore. Close to the sea, the temperature was easier to take.

"Still, strange to be sitting on a beach in the middle of the day," she murmured, then glanced around quickly. Talking to yourself was the first sign of a wandering mind. She sure as heck didn't want witnesses.

If she were back home right now, she'd be rushing down Fifth Avenue, clutching her purse to her side and walking fast enough to keep up with the incredible pulse and rhythm of New York City. She'd be racing from one meeting to the next, lining up volunteers and donations for whichever charitable organization she was working for at the time. There would be luncheons and brunches and coffee-fueled meetings at trendy restaurants.

Busy days and empty nights.

She shivered, took another bite of the hot dog and told herself that her life was full. She did good work—important work. In the grand scheme of things did it really matter that at some point in the last five years, she'd actually stopped *living* her life?

"Great," she muttered, rolling up her napkin and taking a swallow of her soda. "Self-pity party at the pier. Bring your own *whine*."

She pushed off the rock and started for the shoreline where the water edged in across the sand, staining it dark and shining. Terry smiled, kicked off her sandals and let the cool, wet sand slide around her feet. The ocean rippled close and lapped over her skin and she kicked at it idly, sending spray into the air.

When her cell phone rang, she almost ignored it. Then sighing, she reached into her shorts pocket, pulled out her phone and glanced at the number before answering.

"Donna. How's Hawaii?"

"God, it's good to be home for a while," her friend said with a sigh of contentment. Then she added quickly, "Jamie, don't hit your brother with the sand shovel."

Terry chuckled and started walking slowly along the edge of the ocean. The tide rolled in and out again with comforting regularity and the shouts of the children on the beach played a nice counterpoint.

"How's it going there?" Donna asked as soon as the Jamie situation was settled.

"Fine. Business is good."

"And Aidan?"

Terry pulled the phone away from her ear and smirked at it. "You are completely shameless."

"Gee, don't know what you mean."

"Right." Terry laughed. "You're impossible."

"I'm a romantic."

"Who's wasting her time."

"Come on," Donna wheedled. "You've got to admit he's gorgeous."

"He is," Terry admitted with a sigh as an image of Aidan Reilly rose in her mind. "I give you that. But the man swore off sex, remember?"

"Uh-huh. And trust me," Donna said. "He's a man on the edge. Wouldn't take much effort to push him over."

"I thought you were supposed to be *helping* him."

"I'm *trying* to help both of you."

"And it seems so much like interfering."

"To the suspicious mind…"

"Not interested," Terry said firmly and half wondered if she was trying to convince Donna or herself. Then she said it again, just for good measure. "Seriously. Not interested."

"Fine, fine," Donna agreed. "I can see you're going to be stubborn, so forget I said anything."

"Already working on it," Terry assured her and swished one foot through a rush of cold seawater.

From a distance, a shout floated to her and she looked up in time to see a man jump off the pier and drop, feet first, into the ocean below. "What an idiot."

"What? Who are you talking about?"

Shaking her head, Terry said, "Some moron just jumped off the pier."

"That's nuts," Donna screeched. "That close to shore, there are rocks and sandbars and—"

"Now he's swimming to shore, so apparently he survived."

"You know what they say," Donna said, "God protects fools and drunks—Jamie, don't hit your brother with the sand pail, either!"

"Whether he's a fool or drunk is still a mystery," Terry murmured, only half listening to her friend as she kept her gaze locked on the idiot swimming through the waves. "But he's a good swimmer."

When he finally hit shore, he stood up and turned toward her. His dark T-shirt clung to his muscular chest and his sodden cutoff jeans shorts hung from his narrow hips. As she watched, he came closer, grinning now and Terry's stomach fluttered weirdly as she whispered, "I don't believe it."

"What?"

"It's him. Aidan."

"The moron who jumped off the pier?"

"The very one and he's headed this way," Terry said, trying to ignore the stutter of her heart and the jolt in the pit of her stomach.

"Well, well, well," Donna said, laughing, "isn't this fascinating?"

"Go save Danny from Jamie," Terry muttered and hung up while Donna was still laughing.

Stuffing the phone back into her pocket, she gripped her sandals tightly in one fist and waited as Aidan came closer. If she had any sense at all, she'd turn around and head back the way she'd come. Take the stairs up to Main Street and get back to the bookstore.

But simple pride kept her in place.

No way was she going to run away from him. Give him the satisfaction of knowing that he could get to her without even an effort.

"Come here often?" Aidan asked.

"Are you insane?"

His grin widened and her heart did a fast two-step. Ridiculous how this man could jitter her equilibrium.

"Not legally," he said and swiped the water from his face with one tanned, long fingered hand.

His soaking wet shorts hung low across his narrow hips. His legs were long and tan and his feet were bare. He looked athletic, rugged and way too good.

"You jumped off the pier."

"Yeah." He half turned and waved one arm over his head.

Two men on the pier waved back.

"Your keepers?" she asked.

Aidan laughed and turned back to look at her. "My brothers. Well, two of 'em."

Staring at Terry, he could see she was annoyed and damned if she still wasn't an amazing looking woman. Her green eyes flashed at him and disapproval radiated off of her. But there was something else, too…something like excitement. And that made the jump off the pier and the swim to shore more than worthwhile.

He could still hear Connor's and Brian's hoots of glee when he'd spotted Terry and told them to take his fishing gear home for him. No doubt they were already planning to make room for him in the convertible they'd be riding around base come Battle Color Day. But hell with that, Aidan told himself. No way was he going to be seen in public wearing a grass skirt and a coconut bra like his bet-losing brothers.

Nope.

Instead he planned on having a front row seat for the spectacle—cheering them on while basking in the glow of their envy—for him having won the bet.

"The other two thirds of your set of triplets?"

One of his eyebrows lifted. "Donna tell you lots about me or what?"

"Just the basics," Terry said and walked a little further into the ankle deep water. "She never mentioned your death wish."

He threw his head back and laughed. "Death wish? From jumping off that short pier? Babe, that little jump was like rolling off the couch to me."

"What about the rocks? Sandbars?"

He waved her points away and joined her in the froth of water sluicing up over the sand. "From the fourth pylon to the sixth, there's a trench, deeper water. We've been jumping off that stupid pier since we were kids."

"So you've always been crazy."

"Pretty much."

"You grew up here?"

"Ah, so Donna did leave out a few details."

Terry chuckled, glanced at him and gave him a half shrug. "There's that ego again. Contrary to what you may believe, Donna and I didn't really discuss you in great depth."

He laughed again. Something about the way she could quickly go from fury to prickly to laughing really got to him. Nothing like a woman whose moods you couldn't predict to keep a man on his toes.

Not to mention her lushly packed body. It hadn't been hard to spot her from the pier. Her profile was tough to miss. She had more dangerous curves than the Indy 500 and her shoulder-length blond hair flew out around her in the sea wind like a starting flag. Probably every male within miles had already started their engines.

God knew *his* was up and running.

He brushed that thought aside, though. He wasn't some hormone driven teenager with his first case of lust. He could control himself. He could talk to her without drooling all over her. And he'd damn well prove that to both himself and the brothers he *knew* were still watching from the pier.

"Well then," he said and walked closer to her, dragging his feet through the icy froth of water, "let me regale you with tales of the Reilly brothers."

She smiled and shook her head. "So this is a comedy?"

"With us? Damn straight." He shifted his gaze from hers to the endless stretch of ocean laid out in front of them.

The sunlight glittered on the surface of the water, like a spotlight on diamonds. A few sailboats skimmed close to shore, their sails bellied in the wind. Surfers lazily rode the minor swells in toward shore and overhead, seagulls danced and screeched. A couple of kids with swim floats raced in and out of the water while their parents watched from a blanket and from not too far away, came the tinny sound of country music sliding from a radio.

"We moved to Baywater when we were thirteen. Liam was fifteen. Our dad was a Marine, so up until then, we'd traveled all over the damn place." He smiled when he said it, remembering all the moves with a lot more fondness than his mother felt for them. "We were stationed in Germany, Okinawa, California and even a quick stint in Hawaii."

"All before you were thirteen?"

"Yep." The water was cold, the sun was hot and a gorgeous woman was standing beside him. Days just didn't get any better than this. "Anyway, when he was assigned to MCAS Beaufort—"

"MCAS?"

He grinned. "Sorry. Marines tend to talk in acronyms. MCAS. Marine Corps Air Station."

"Ah…" She nodded.

"When he was assigned there, we followed just like always. He made every move seem like an adventure. New town, new friends, new school."

She was quiet for a minute or two, then looked up at him with eyes that looked deep. "Must have been hard."

"Could have been," he admitted, caught for a moment or two by the empathy in her eyes. But he didn't need her sympathy. "Probably was for other Marine brats. But we always had each other. So we'd go into a new school with built-in friends."

"Handy."

More than handy, he thought. The Reilly brothers had stuck together through thick and thin. Even when they were battling—which was pretty damn often— there was a bond between the four of them that had been stronger than any outside pressure.

"Hey, there's a lot to be said for having a big family. Always someone to hang with."

"Or fight with?"

"Oh, yeah. We had some great ones. Still do on occasion. You have brothers and sisters?"

"One," she said. "Brother. Older. We're not close."

There was a story there that she wasn't telling. He could see it in the way she shifted slightly away from him. Her body language said a hell of a lot more than she was. "Why not?"

She stiffened a little further, lifted her chin as if

preparing for a battle that she was used to fighting. Then she said, "Lots of reasons. But we weren't talking about me, remember?"

Shut down. Neatly. Politely. Completely. Okay. He'd let it go, he thought. Come back to it another time. He wanted to know why her green eyes looked shadowed. Why her brow furrowed at mention of her family. And yet…he really didn't want to explore *why* he wanted to know.

So he was happy enough to turn the talk back to him and his family.

For now.

"Right." He blew out a breath, focused on the sea again and started talking. "Anyway, Mom handled everything, as usual. Dad made it an adventure, Mom made it all work. She handled the packing, the bills, the requisitions, the dealing with the movers…everything. Basically all us guys had to do was show up."

"Your mother's crazy, too," she said, though her words were filled with more than a little admiration.

He laughed shortly. "She'd be the first to agree with that." He shrugged and stared hard at the horizon, where sea met sky and both blended, becoming a part of each other. "But, everything changed when we moved here. Mom loved it. Said she felt a 'connection' to this place. She loved everything about Beaufort, the south, the people. When she found Baywater on a shopping trip, she told my dad that here is where they'd be staying."

"Could he do that? Just opt to stop being deployed?"

"Not easy, but, yeah. Ask for an assignment to a company that doesn't deploy and you're pretty safe. But Mom wouldn't let him do that. She knew how much he enjoyed the deployments."

"But what about when he was reassigned to live somewhere else for a year or two? That happens, doesn't it?"

"You bet. Mom just told him 'happy trails' and that she'd be right here, letting us go to school and have some stability." He shoved both hands into his jeans pockets and winced as he realized he'd dived into the water still carrying his wallet. Damn it. But he hadn't been thinking. He'd taken one look at Terry and jumped off the pier.

He shook his head. "Mom wanted us to be able to finish out high school in the same place."

"So she stayed here with you guys and let him go?"

"Yep." He smiled to himself. "Dad would head off for six months and Mom would be right here, running the show until he got back. She told him this was home and she wasn't leaving it again."

"Strong woman."

"You have *no* idea." He laughed, remembering how his mother had managed to ride herd on four teenage sons and make it all look easy. "Dad lasted another year or two, then wangled an assignment back to MCAS and they've been here ever since. He retired not long after that—"

"Now?"

Aidan sighed. "He died a few years back."

"I'm sorry."

He looked at her. "Thanks. Mom's still in their house here in Baywater and loving the fact that all three of her sons are stationed close enough for her to irritate whenever she wants to."

"And you're all nuts about her."

He shrugged. "Hard not to be."

"And your other brother?"

"Ah, Liam. *Father* Liam." Aidan looked down at her, then lifted one hand to tuck a long strand of silky blond hair behind her ear. "Every Irish woman's dream is to be able to say, 'my son the priest.' Liam's church, St. Sebastian's, is here in town, too, so Mom lucked out. For a while anyway. Until one of us is transferred out."

"Even apart, though, you'll still have each other."

He studied her and noticed the shadows were back, haunting her eyes. Something inside him wanted to reassure her. To wipe away the shadows and make her smile.

And that worried the hell out of him.

Four

By late afternoon, the wind had picked up, the sky was crowded with clouds and Terry was still trying to convince herself that Aidan wasn't getting to her.

But he was.

"Damn it."

She closed the shop, locked the door behind her and stepped out onto the sidewalk. Tilting her head back, she watched the slate-gray clouds colliding into each other like bumper cars gone amuck.

"Storm coming." A soft voice, female, with just a touch of humor in it.

Terry turned, smiling, to face Selma Wyatt. At least seventy years old, Selma's blue eyes sparkled with a kind of vitality that Terry envied. The woman's long, silver hair hung in one thick, neat braid, across the shoulder of her gauzy, pale yellow, ankle skimming dress. The toes of her purple sneakers peeked from beneath the hem.

"Yeah," Terry said with another quick look skyward. "Sure looks like it."

Selma shook her head until that thick braid swung out like a pendulum. "Not the storm I'm talking about, honey."

"Ah…" Terry nodded sagely and didn't bother to hide her smile. "See something interesting in your cards?"

The older woman ran the spirit shop/palm reader emporium next door. And though Terry had never been one to believe in the whole "mystic" thing, she figured Selma must be good at what she did, because there was an almost constant stream of customers coming and going from the Spirit Shop all day long.

In the few days Terry had been in town, Selma had pretty much adopted her. She'd taken her out to lunch, introduced her to the noontime crowd at Delilah's diner and pretty much elected herself friend and watchdog. She'd even offered to give Terry a "reading," but she'd declined, since, if her future was anything like her past…Terry really didn't want to know.

"Heck no, honey," Selma said. "Didn't need the cards for this one. It's in the air. Can't you feel it?"

A slight chill danced up Terry's spine before she shook it off, telling herself that Selma'd been staring into her crystal ball too long. "The only storm I feel is the one blowing in off the ocean."

Selma smiled patiently—the same kind of smile an adult gave a two-year-old who insists on tying his own shoe even though he can't quite manage it. "Of course, dear. Pay no attention to me." Then she paused, cocked her head and said, "Oh. There it is. Wait for it."

A little impatient now and feeling just a bit uneasy, Terry inhaled sharply and asked, "Wait for what?"

Then she heard it.

A low rumble of sound.

Like distant thunder, it growled and roared as it came closer. The fine hairs at the back of Terry's neck lifted and she turned her head toward the sound.

Overhead, lightning shimmered behind the clouds, just a warning. A hint of bigger things to come.

But she forgot all about the storm as she watched a huge motorcycle slink to the curb and stop. In the dim light of dusk, the spotless chrome sparkled and shone and the black paint gleamed like fresh sin.

And speaking of sin…

Aidan Reilly sat astride the motorcycle and dropped both booted feet to the ground to steady the bike while he looked at her.

"Now *that's* a storm, honey," Selma murmured. "A big one."

Terry hardly heard her. Her breath came fast and short. Her heartbeat jittered unsteadily and every cell in her body caught fire at once.

He wore faded jeans and the battered cowboy boots he'd had on the first day she met him. His black T-shirt was strained across his chest, looking about two sizes too small—not that she was complaining. He wore dark glasses that hid his eyes from her, but no helmet and he looked…*dangerous*.

Her stomach fisted and she swallowed hard against the gigantic knot of something hot and needy lodged in her throat.

Then he smiled and Terry felt her toes curl.

Oh, this couldn't be good.

"Evening, Ms. Wyatt," he said, his voice as low and rumbly as the engine of the machine vibrating beneath him.

"Aidan," Selma said with a nod and a smile. "Come to have your fortune read?"

He grinned. "Now, Ms. Wyatt, you know I like surprises."

"Then I'll leave you to them," she said and headed off down the sidewalk.

Terry barely registered the fact that the woman was gone. All she could think was, it just wasn't fair for a man to look that good.

And why did he have to have a motorcycle?

"Terry!"

She blinked her way out of a very interesting daydream and realized that he must have been calling her name for a couple of minutes. How embarrassing was *that*?

Burying her own jittery reaction to him under a snarl of much more comfortable indignation, she snapped, "What're you doing here, Aidan?"

He glanced at the sky just as a grumble of thunder rolled out, long and low, and filled with the promise of coming rain. Then he glanced back at her. "Just thought maybe you could use a ride back to Donna's house."

"I can walk," she said, turning to put action to the words. The faster she got some distance between she and Aidan, the better, all the way around. "Thanks anyway."

He kept pace with her, rolling the bike and walking it down the side of the street with his long legs. "Gonna rain any time now," he pointed out.

"Then I'd better hurry," she countered, telling herself to put one foot in front of the other. To keep moving. To for heaven's sake, don't *look* at him.

He chuckled. "You're so stubborn you'd rather get wet than accept a ride from me?"

She chanced a quick glance at him. "Hello? On a motorcycle, I'd get wet anyway."

"Yeah," he pointed out with a quick grin that showed off the dimple she'd been spending too much time thinking about, "but you'd be moving faster. Having more fun."

"Slow can be fun, too," she said tightly and wondered why she suddenly sounded like a ninety-year-old librarian.

"I grant you. In some things, slow is *way* better."

She stumbled when the images *that* remark blossomed in full, glorious color in her brain. Oh, God. Did his voice just drop another notch, or was she simply going deaf from the pounding of her own heartbeat? Swallowing hard, she demanded, "Don't you have to be somewhere?"

"I'm right where I want to be."

"And what about the bet?" she asked hotly, stopping short to face him.

He lifted one eyebrow, took off his dark glasses and hooked them in the collar of his shirt. "Babe. I asked you to ride the motorcycle—didn't ask you to ride *me*."

A quick rush of heat swamped Terry and she wondered if everyone was seeing those little black dots now fluttering in her vision—or if it was just her. Probably just her. Which couldn't be a good sign.

Taking a deep breath, she got a good tight hold on suddenly rampaging hormones and told herself to get over it. She wasn't looking for a fling and if she were, she wouldn't be looking at Aidan Reilly. The man had sworn off the very thing she was suddenly hungry for. So what point was there in getting herself whipped up into a frenzy?

None.

So okay, she could do this. She could be a grown-up. And besides…a fat, solitary raindrop splattered on top of her head. He had a point. If he took her home on that rolling sex machine, then she'd be in out of the rain a lot faster than she would be if she was stubborn and insisted on walking.

This was purely an act of necessity.

Nothing out of the ordinary to accept a ride from a friend of a friend.

He was just doing her a favor.

Not the favor she secretly *wanted,* but he didn't have to know that.

"Okay," she said, trying to shut up the internal argument she was having with herself. "I'll take the ride. Thanks."

He gave her a slow smile that set fire to the soles of her feet, but she refused to feel the flames. As the rain spattered around her, she walked to the bike. He reached back and unstrapped a shiny black helmet from the tall, chrome backrest bar.

"Good," he said, handing it to her. "Put this on."

"Why do I have to wear a helmet and you don't?" she asked, taking the darn thing.

"Because my head's a lot harder than yours."

"Don't bet on it," she muttered, but yanked the helmet on and fixed the strap under her chin.

"Looks good on you."

"Oh, I'm sure," she said and swung her left leg over the seat as she climbed aboard. Good thing she'd worn linen shorts to work today instead of a skirt.

He half turned to look at her. "Grab hold of my waist and hang on."

Oh, boy.

Beneath her, the powerful engine throbbed and purred as he gunned the motor. The resulting vibrations of the bike set up a series of trembling quivers inside her that took her to the brink of something really interesting.

And she hadn't even touched him yet.

"Are you going to hang on or what?"

She gritted her teeth and grabbed hold of his waist. She didn't have to wrap her arms around him or anything. A simple handhold would be enough, she told herself and fought the rush of something hot and dark and sweet as he revved the engine again and eased the bike onto the street.

The stoplight at the corner was red, so they didn't go far.

She heard the smile in his voice as he glanced back over his shoulder and said, "You're gonna have to get a better grip on me than *that*."

"I'm fine," she insisted, trying not to think about her thighs aligned along his or the powerful engine vibrating beneath her.

"What's wrong, babe? I *worry* you?"

"Not at all. Why don't you just take care of driving and I'll take care of me."

"Your call." He shrugged, turned his face forward again and when the light blinked to green, he took off like the hounds of hell were right behind them.

"Hey!" She shrieked and instinctively wrapped both arms around his middle.

He chuckled and she felt his body shake with silent laughter.

Let him laugh, she thought. She was more interested in keeping her perch on the bike than she was in pretending to be aloof.

He steered the bike down Main street, threading between the cars chugging lazily along the road. As they picked up speed, the wind slapped at her, raindrops pelted her like tiny bullets of ice and Terry relaxed enough to smile, enjoying the rush of air, the sense of freedom and the small, tingling sensation of danger.

It had been so long.

Before her life had become one charitable function after another, she had sought out things like this. Motorcycles, paragliding, deep sea dives, rock climbing.

She hadn't always been adventurous—but when her world collapsed, Terry had stopped caring. She'd gone out of her way to *live* every moment. She'd sought out the most exciting, the most heart pounding, risky activities she could find and then lost herself—and her pain—in the adrenaline rush.

Until five years ago.

When she'd awakened in a hospital one morning, to find herself lying there with a broken arm and leg. And she'd finally realized that chasing death wasn't living. That burying her pain didn't make it disappear. And that the only way to make that pain livable was to help people however she could.

Since that morning, she'd become a champion of causes. Terry Evans became the "go to" girl for most charitable foundations in and around Manhattan. She arranged flashy fund-raisers, was able to browbeat bazillionaires into contributions they'd never had any intention of making and could turn a celebrity auction into the event of the year. And she did it all with a calm, cool smile that managed to hide the *real* Terry from almost everyone.

She had legions of acquaintances, but very few *friends*. And the friends she *did* have, were more her family than those she was related to by blood.

Which was how she'd ended up in Baywater, South Carolina, sitting behind a hunk in jeans, riding a motorcycle in the rain.

Because of Donna.

Since that awful moment twelve years ago, when Terry's world dropped out from under her, Donna had been there for her. She'd cried with her, hugged her and supported her when Terry had taken her stand against her family. Donna Fletcher was the one link to her past that Terry treasured.

"How you doin' back there?"

Aidan's shout cut into her thoughts and Terry inhaled sharply, reminding herself that the past was long gone. "I'm fine," she called back, to be heard over the roar of the engine.

Rain still spattered, as if the storm just couldn't work up the energy to get serious. As they roared along the road, streetlights winked into life and the few raindrops falling were spotlighted in the glow.

A car whizzed past, its radio blaring, tires spitting up water in its wake. Terry ducked her head behind Aidan's shoulder and stared out to one side as the storefronts gave way to houses and those to trees lining the coast road.

The throb of the engine beneath her, the rush of wind all around her, her arms around Aidan's hard middle and the cool splat of rain against her skin, was mesmerizing. Which was why it took her an extra minute or two to notice something.

"Hey!" she shouted, lifting her head. "You missed the turn to Donna's street."

"No, I didn't."

"You passed it."

"Yes, but I didn't *miss* it."

She squeezed her arms tight around him and he grunted. "What're you up to?"

"Can't you just enjoy the ride?" he asked.

"Not until you tell me what's going on." Damn it. She'd relaxed her guard. She never should have taken this ride from him. She'd known it was a mistake the minute she climbed onto the bike. But what red-blooded woman would have been able to say "no" to a Marine cowboy biker?

"Aidan…"

"Relax, babe—"

"Stop calling me *babe*."

He laughed. She felt it shake through him and it made her grit her teeth even harder. The minute he stopped this bike, she was jumping off and *walking* if she had to, back to Donna's house.

The magic of the ride was gone as she simmered quietly in a temper that flashed and flared inside her. By the time he finally *did* stop the bike, Terry didn't even pause to see where they were before she leapt off her perch, snatched off her helmet and glared at him.

"You really *are* nuts, aren't you?"

He grinned at her and she realized that sexy or not, that smile could get really irritating.

"Thought you might like to take a little sightseeing tour."

"In the *rain?*"

He held out one hand palm up and shrugged. "We drove out of the rain a few minutes ago."

Frowning, Terry lifted her face to the sky and saw that he was right. They'd driven far enough out of Baywater that they'd left the brief summer storm behind them. Now, she took a minute and glanced around. She stood on a cliff road, the ocean far below them. The road behind them was nearly deserted and lined by towering trees that dipped and swayed in the wind as if dancing to a tune only they could hear.

When she finally turned to look at Aidan again, she found him standing beside her, staring out over the black water. Moonlight peeked out from behind the clouds, darting in and out of shadows, like a child playing hide-and-seek.

"Worth the ride?" he asked.

She shifted her gaze to the view and had to admit, it was gorgeous. Moonlight danced on the water, then winked out of existence when the clouds scudded across the surface of the moon. Whitecaps dazzled with phosphorescence that looked ghostly in the darkness.

"It's beautiful."

"One of my favorite spots," he said, walking closer to the edge of the cliff, until he could curl his hands around the top bar of the iron guard rail. "I come up here when I need to get away from people for a while."

She joined him, taking slow, almost reluctant steps. "Then you really shouldn't bring *people* with you."

He glanced at her and shrugged. "Usually don't."

Idly she swung the helmet in her left hand, slapping it gently against her thigh. "So why me?"

"Interesting question."

"That's not an answer."

He turned his back on the view and faced her, leaning against the railing and crossing his arms over his chest. "Don't have one," he admitted after a long moment.

His blue eyes fixed on her, Terry had to force herself to stand still beneath his steady regard. She didn't want to think about the subtle licks of warmth invading the pit of her stomach. She *did* want to hold onto her temper, but it was already fading.

"I just wanted to see you again."

"Why?"

He laughed shortly. "Beats the hell outta me."

"Aidan," she said on a sigh, "this isn't a good idea."

"Which idea is that?"

"This," she said, waving one arm even as she gripped the helmet in one tight fist. *"Us.* You. Me."

"Well that about covers everything," he said, still smiling, "except for what I feel when I'm around you."

"Aidan…"

"You feel it, too."

Oh, boy howdy.

But that wasn't the point.

"Doesn't really matter what we feel, does it?" She tipped her chin up and stared at him, unwilling to let him know just how close she was to losing control.

"Why not?"

"Because whatever it is, it's based on hormones."

"And your problem with that is…?"

"For heaven's sake, Aidan, we're not high school kids."

"What's that got to do with anything?"

Think, she told herself. But all the urging in the world wasn't quite enough to kick-start her brain when her body was obviously in charge, here.

Shaking his head, Aidan spoke again. "There's something here, Terry. Between us."

"There can't be," she said.

He laughed and the low, throaty sound rolled over her with a warmth that dispelled the chill wind. "Why the hell not?"

"Your stupid *bet,* for one thing."

He blew that off with a wave of his hand. "I'm not talking about sex."

That stopped her.

"You're not?"

"Was that disappointment I heard in your voice?" he asked.

"Of course not," she covered quickly. "Just…confusion."

His eyebrows wiggled. "Well, let me clear things up for you. I haven't forgotten about the bet. A little less than three weeks to go and I'm the champion Reilly."

"And that's important to you?"

"Damn straight. I want to be able to lord it over my brothers forever."

"That's mature."

He shrugged and smiled. "*Anyway,* I wasn't talking about sex before, Terry. Though it appears I am now, and can I just say, I'm happy to hear you bring it up?"

"Cut it out," she said and tossed the helmet to him. He caught it neatly. "You don't want to lose a bet and I'm not looking for a summer fling."

"Oh, I'm not going to lose the bet," he said and

pushed away from the rail to walk toward her. "And I'm not looking to be your 'fling,' either."

"Good."

"But…"

"No buts…"

"But…" He repeated as he walked closer, keeping pace even as she inched back warily. "There's lots of things two people can do without actually having sex."

"This is *so* not a conversation I want to have."

"Then we're on the same page after all."

"What?" The wind raced past her, tossing her hair across her eyes and Terry frantically reached up to push it away. Wouldn't pay to take her gaze off him. He was just too smooth to *not* keep an eye on.

He tossed the helmet toward the bike and watched it roll until it came to a stop on the ground beside the front wheel. Then he shifted his gaze back to her, stepped up close and grabbed her hips in a hard, two-fisted grip.

"Aidan…"

"Terry…" He bent his head, smiled and whispered, "Shut up," just before he kissed her.

Five

He groaned as his mouth came down over hers.

Aidan hadn't planned to kiss her.

Hell, if it came to that, he hadn't planned to *see* her tonight. When he left the base, he'd headed straight for the Off Duty, a local bar that catered to Marines. He'd had a beer, and shot a game of pool with a First Sergeant who had more money than pool playing ability. He'd joked around with a few of his friends, bought a round of drinks for a gunnery sergeant about to be deployed—and then he left. Hadn't been able to sit there talking shop with the guys because his mind was somewhere else.

With Terry Evans.

The damn woman had been in his brain all day. Her face had haunted him. Her smile had tempted him. Her temper intrigued him. Since earlier that afternoon, when he'd jumped off the pier to see her—she'd been with him. And he hadn't been able to shake her, despite his efforts.

Now, with his mouth on hers, Aidan felt her slip even deeper inside him.

The taste of her, the feel of her against him, swamped him with more sensations than he'd ever experienced before.

And he wanted more.

He held her tighter to him, wrapping his arms around her middle, sliding his hands up and down her back, following the line of her spine, cupping the curve of her behind.

Her mouth opened under his and his tongue swept within, exploring, defining, discovering her secrets, reveling in the rush of sensations rippling through him.

She sighed into his mouth and her breath filled him. He swallowed it and demanded more. His arms tightened around her further, squeezing until she moaned against him and he could have sworn he felt the imprint of her body on his.

And still it wasn't enough.

Too many weeks of celibacy, he thought wildly, while he tore his mouth from hers to run his lips and tongue along the column of her throat. Too long without the taste of a woman, without the feel of her heat. That's all this was. A reaction to deprivation.

"No," he murmured, running the tip of his tongue across her skin until she shivered and grabbed at his shoulders. That wasn't all. He'd been horny before. He'd been needy before. And he'd never known such an all encompassing hunger. He didn't just *want*.

He wanted *her*.

"Aidan…"

He barely heard her whisper over the roaring in his ears. His heartbeat thundered in his chest and his blood pumped with a blinding passion that left him breathless.

"Aidan…"

Groggily, like a man waking up from a three-day drunk, Aidan lifted his head and stared down at her. "Terry—" He touched her face, running his fingertips down her cheek. She closed her eyes and shuddered in an unsteady breath.

"This is *not* good," she finally said, in a voice so soft, a freshening wind nearly carried it away.

He forced a short laugh. "I don't know. I thought it was *damn* good."

"That's not what I meant," she said and stepped back, away from him.

His hand fell to his side and he fisted it, as if to capture the feel of her skin on his fingertips. Already, he wanted to be touching her again. Already, he missed the taste of her. Warning bells clanged in the back of his brain, but Aidan ignored them. His heart-beat was still racing and his breathing way less than steady.

From below them, came the thunderous, pulsing roar of the ocean as breakers smashed into the rocks. Out on the highway, a solitary car streamed by, its engine whining briefly before disappearing into the darkness. And here on the cliff's edge, an icy wind swept past them, around them,

Drawing them together and at the same time, holding them apart.

"Look, Aidan," she said, lifting both hands to shove her wind-tousled hair back from her face, "I just think that this is...*dangerous.*"

He gave her a quick grin. "Nothing wrong with a little danger. It spices things up."

A quick, harsh laugh shot from her throat. "Oh, man," she said, turning away from him to stare out over the ocean, "it's probably a good thing we didn't meet five years ago."

Intrigued, he stepped up beside her and tried not to notice when she inched away from him. "Why five years ago?"

She glanced at him and in the pale wash of moonlight, her blue eyes shone. "Back then," she said softly, "I'd have given you a run for your money, dangerwise."

"Yeah?" He smiled down at her, even as her features shuttered and her own smile faded.

She shifted her gaze back to the water and took the step or two that brought her close to the iron guardrail. She closed her hands over the top rung, lifted her face into the wind and said, "Yeah. Parasailing, deep sea dives, mountain climbing…"

"You? Danger girl?" He grinned as he stared at her, trying to imagine her racing through life looking for an adrenaline rush. Nope. He just couldn't picture it.

"It was a long time ago."

"Sounds like fun."

"It was. For a while."

Aidan leaned one hip against the top railing, folded his arms over his chest and watched her, thoughtfully now. "What changed?"

She leaned forward, straining toward the ocean as if trying to escape the conversation. "*I* changed."

"A shame."

Glancing at him, she smiled briefly. "You *would* think so."

He shrugged. "Nothing wrong with chasing life at high speed."

"I suppose," she said softly. "Unless it's not about chasing as much as it is about running."

"From what?"

He wanted to know, even though a part of him wondered how this conversation had taken such a turn. A minute ago, he'd held her in his arms, tasted her breath, captured her sighs, felt her tremble in his grasp. Now, she was standing just inches from him and yet, it felt as though she were miles away.

"Life?" One word, more of a question than a statement.

Misery etched itself onto her features and even in the dim light of a nearly cloud covered moon, Aidan saw the shadows crouched in her eyes. He wanted to reach for her, but something told him she wouldn't welcome the contact.

Not now.

"You want to talk about it?"

She looked at him again, seemed to consider it, then said, "No. I don't."

Disappointment rose up inside him and surprised the hell out of Aidan. He'd wanted to know what put the shadows in her eyes. What it was that had such power over her that years later, just the memory of it could bring pain strong enough to make her shudder with it.

Always before, he'd kept his relationships on a superficial level. It was, he'd always assured himself, where he felt most comfortable. He wasn't looking to find a happily ever after. He wasn't looking for Ms. Right—more like Ms. Right *Now.*

He'd never really bought into the whole concept of being married to one person for*ever.* There were just too many women and not enough time as far as Aidan was concerned. He liked his action hot and his women temporary. And that outlook on life had served him well so far.

Didn't matter that his brothers—fellow triplets—had just lately fallen into the cozy clutches of two great women. Hell, he didn't mind being the last Reilly standing. He'd go through life proudly carrying the Bachelor banner.

So why then, did he suddenly want to know Terry Evans's secrets? Why did he *care* about whatever it was making her sad? It wasn't any of his business. Shouldn't affect him.

And yet...

"I really think you should take me home, now," she said, splintering his thoughts with the effectiveness of a hand grenade.

Probably best, he thought, but heard himself ask, "Still running?"

She stiffened and narrowed her eyes.

Well, great. Way to go, Aidan. Nice job.

He held up both hands and gave her a smile. "Never mind. Stupid thing to say."

"Fine. Can we go now?"

"Sure." He pushed away from the railing, took her elbow in a firm grip and steered her the few steps toward the bike. Bending down, he scooped up the helmet, then handed it to her.

She took it in both hands, and staring at it as if she'd never seen it before, she said, "Look, Aidan, about that kiss..."

He swung his left leg over the bike and settled onto the seat. Looking up at her, he gave her a smile he figured she needed about now. "Just a kiss, babe. Not a world ender."

"Right," she said and pulled the helmet on. She buckled the strap, then climbed onto the bike behind him.

"Just a kiss."

Her thighs aligned along his.

Her arms came around his waist.

Her breasts pressed into his back.

Aidan fired up the engine and revved it hard, gritting his teeth as he steered the bike out onto the road and back toward the storm hovering over Baywater.

Oh, yeah.

Just a kiss.

No problem.

"So what's the problem?"

Aidan glared at his older brother, then threw the basketball at him. "Haven't you been listening?"

Liam laughed, took the ball and bounced it idly, keeping one eye on the ball and one eye on his brother. "You mean to the rambling story you've been telling me for the last hour and a half? Yes. I was listening."

Aidan muttered a curse, bent down and snatched up a water bottle from the side of the driveway behind St. Sebastian's church. Uncapping it, he took a long drink, hoping the still cold water would put out some of the fires that had been with him since he dropped Terry off at Donna's house the night before.

It didn't.

And the weather wasn't helping any, either. Hot. Hot and humid, with the air so damn thick, it felt as though you should chew it before inhaling. Roiling gray clouds moved sluggishly across the sky and a hot wind occasionally kicked up out of nowhere. Hurricane season in the south.

Aidan exhaled sharply and narrowed his eyes on the sky. He had a feeling in his bones that the hurricane even now building up in the ocean would be headed their way all too soon. Which meant that the Search and Rescue unit would be on high alert twenty-four hours a day—not just for sea rescues, but working with the local police as well. In times of emergency, people didn't care *who* saved them—as long as they got saved.

Ordinarily the Coast Guard would take up a lot of the slack when it came to disaster time. But here, just outside Beaufort, the closest Coast Guard unit was stationed in Savannah and no one was going to sit around and wait for help. He squinted as the sun briefly peeped out from behind a bank of clouds and thought about the last hurricane that had blown through just a month ago.

Baywater was lucky that time around. Got plenty of rain and enough wind to snatch off shutters and toss old trees. But nothing as devastating as the outer banks had seen. He hoped their luck would hold.

"Worried about the storm?" Liam asked, drawing Aidan out of his thoughts.

"A little," he said, shrugging. "Weather report says it's going to skip us this time, hit in North Carolina. But my bones tell me different."

Liam nodded and glanced skyward. "I hate hoping for disaster to visit someone else."

"You're not. You're just doing what everyone else is doing and hoping it skips *us*."

Aidan recapped the water bottle, tossed it onto the grass under the shade of an oak tree and snapped another look at Liam. "So back to the point…where's the advice, *Father?* You're a priest, for God's sake. Say something meaningful."

Liam chuckled, turned on one heel and jumped, firing the basketball at the hoop tacked up over the garage behind the rectory. *Swish.* The ball swept through the net without ever touching the rim of the basket. Grinning, he trotted up to retrieve the ball, then tossed it back to his brother. "What kind of advice did you have in mind, Aidan?"

"Something *comforting,* damn it."

Liam laughed again. "Since when do you need comfort on the subject of women?"

This couldn't get much more humiliating, so he spilled his guts. "Since a few days ago, all right?" Hadn't he just spent the last hour or so explaining all of this?

"Donna's friend Terry is getting to you."

"I didn't say that."

"Sure you did."

No. He deliberately had *not* said that. In fact, he'd talked circles around himself in an effort to stay far away from such a statement. Apparently, though, Liam was good enough at reading his brothers that he didn't need a flat out admission.

"What do you want me to say, Aidan?"

"I don't know. You're the priest. Come up with something."

Liam laughed, bounced the basketball a couple of times, then shot it at his brother. Aidan snatched it and held on to it with a viselike grip.

All night, he'd thought about Terry. About that kiss. About the way she'd looked up at him in the moonlight. About those damn shadows in her eyes. And all night, he'd kicked himself for not staying with her. For not digging out what it was she didn't want to talk about.

Which was just so unusual for him, he'd shown up at the church at the crack of dawn for a little sympathy from the family priest. So far, he hadn't gotten much more than his butt kicked in a game of Horse.

Liam walked to where he'd dropped his own bottle of cold water, grabbed it and glugged down half of it before speaking again. "Aidan, you're just shook up because you've never been interested in a woman beyond getting her into your bed before."

Aidan stared at him. "That's it? That's the best you've got? They teach you that at priest school?"

"You're not mad at me, you know," Liam said, capping the bottle again and tossing it to the lawn.

"Really? Cause I think I am."

"You're mad at *you.*"

"That's brilliant. For this I got up early and came over here." Nodding, he tossed the ball back to Liam, then bent to snatch up his T-shirt. Dragging it over his head, he shoved his arms through the sleeves and glared at his older brother again.

"Don't you want to know *why* you're mad at yourself?"

"Enlighten me."

"Because you care about her. And you don't want to."

That was a little close to home, but he wasn't going to give Liam the satisfaction of admitting it. "Don't build this up into some hearts-and-flowers deal. I've only known her a few days."

Liam shrugged and used the hem of his sleeveless jersey to wipe sweat off his forehead. "There's a time limit?"

He snorted. "You're way off base here."

"Sure."

"Seriously." Aidan bounced the basketball again, listening to the solid slap of the ball against the pavement, concentrating on the smack of the ball against his palms. "There's nothing going on between us."

Beyond some amazing sexual chemistry and some curiosity on his part.

"So why're you here?"

"Believe me, I'm kicking myself for coming."

Liam grinned. "You want to know what I think as long as its what you *want* me to think."

"You know," Aidan snarled with a shake of his head, "why we come to you for advice on women is beyond me, anyway. You haven't had a date in fifteen years."

"And you've never been a priest, yet you always feel free to complain about the church."

"Good point."

"But, whether you want this advice or not, I'm going to give it to you." Liam came closer, took the ball from Aidan and bounced it a couple of times while he gathered his thoughts.

Finally he looked at his brother and said, "You've got an opportunity here, Aidan."

"And what's that?"

"You've got the chance to get to know a woman *outside* your bed. Who knows? Maybe you'll like her."

"I do like her." He scowled slightly as those words shot from him before he could keep them bottled up inside where they belonged.

Liam smiled. "Maybe there's hope for you yet, Aidan."

"Yeah, yeah," he muttered and grabbed the ball back from his brother, bouncing it idly a few times while he tried to figure out just when he'd started *liking* Terry Evans.

"So. You gonna last the rest of the bet?"

He snapped his gaze up to meet Liam's. "Damn straight I am."

"Uh-huh." Liam caught the ball on a bounce and backed up, still dribbling. "But just so you know, I picked up Connor's and Brian's grass skirts and co-conut bras the other day."

Well that cheered him right up. Aidan laughed, picturing his brothers, mortified, driving around in a convertible while every Marine in the south was free to laugh their asses off at the Reilly brothers. "Excellent."

"And just in case," Liam said, taking a shot for the hoop, "I picked up a set for *you*, too."

He stiffened. "Not a chance, Liam. No way is that going to happen."

"We'll see about that, won't we? Still have a cou-ple of weeks to go…"

Before Aidan could argue, thunder rolled, grimly, determinedly and the leaves on the trees rattled as a sharp wind blasted through. Aidan glanced up at the sky, watched the gray clouds gathering.

"What do you think?"

"I think we might not get lucky this time."

"Could be days yet before we know."

"Yeah."

"You on call?" Liam asked, teasing forgotten.

"Hurricane season? Always." Hopefully the hur-ricane would burn itself out before reaching them, but even if the full brunt of the storm didn't hit Bay-water, the accompanying winds and drenching rain could do plenty of damage.

"Hard to believe anyone would want to take a boat out in weather like this," Liam was saying.

But Aidan knew differently. Folks never figured that bad things would happen to *them*. It was always the "other" guy who ended up with his picture in the paper.

"Oh, there's always some idiot who thinks a storm warning is for everybody *else* in the city." He grabbed the ball back from Liam and ran three long strides before leaping at the hoop and dunking the ball.

Liam caught the rebound and made a jump of his own as Aidan said, "I guarantee you, right now, there's some guy out on the ocean who never should have left his house."

Six

She should never have left the house.

"Damn it!" Terry turned the ignition key again and listened with disgust to the pitiful whinewhinewhine of an engine trying to start—and failing.

She slammed one fist onto the dash, then gripped the wheel with both hands, squeezing it tightly instead of tearing her own hair out. "I don't believe this," she muttered, lifting her gaze to stare out over the wind-whipped ocean.

She scooped her hair back out of her eyes and stared off in the direction of Baywater. She couldn't see land. A sinking sensation opened up in the pit of her stomach—and she only hoped the boat wouldn't start feeling the same thing. The stupid boat *had* managed to get a few miles out to sea before the engine gave up and sputtered an ugly death. Now she could only pray that the hull of the damn thing was in better shape than its motor.

"What were you thinking?" Good question, but she didn't have a good answer.

She'd been up all night, trying to sleep but unable to close her eyes without being sucked back into the vortex of emotions that Aidan Reilly had stirred inside her. It had all started with the roar and grumble of that damned motorcycle. And sitting behind him, pressed close to his hard, warm body hadn't helped anything.

It had been so long since she'd experienced that flash of awareness, that spark of...*adventure.* She'd believed herself past the need or the desire for those feelings, but once awakened, she hadn't been able to put them to rest again.

She wanted to curse him for it.

But a part of her was grateful.

And then there was that *kiss.* She closed her eyes now and let herself feel it again. That amazing, soul-stirring, heart-crashing, bone-melting kiss. Every inch of her body had jumped to attention and clamored for more. He'd stirred something within her even more intriguing than that quest for adventure. Aidan Reilly had made her remember just how long it had been since she'd felt...*anything.*

She opened her eyes again and sighed as she scanned the ocean, unsuccessfully, for a hint of another boat. Someone she could wave down for assistance. She was, however, *alone*.

And it was all Aidan Reilly's fault.

Just before dawn, Terry had given up on sleep and surrendered to the urge driving her to get up and do something. She'd made her way down to the harbor, found a boat rental place and slapped down enough cash to allow her to steer her own course for a few hours.

That's all she'd wanted. To get out onto the ocean. To feel the wind in her face, the salt spray against her skin. To feel... *free*.

"Of course, it would have helped if the stupid boat would run." Muttering curses, she flipped the radio on, picked up the handset and said, "Mayday, mayday." She let up on the button and listened. Nothing. Not even static. She switched channels, spinning the dial as if it were a wheel of fortune.

Still nothing.

Why she was surprised, she couldn't say. If the engine didn't run, why should the radio work?

Oh, she really was an idiot. She hadn't thought this through. Hadn't checked the boat over before setting out. Hadn't done a damn thing to help herself.

Then she remembered her cell phone. Giving up on the radio, she rummaged in her brown leather shoulder bag and came up with a tiny, flip-top phone.

Sighing, she did the only thing she could do and dialed nine-one-one.

"911, what's the nature of your emergency?"

God, it felt good to hear a voice that wasn't her own. "Hi. This is Terry Evans. I'm stranded in the ocean, a few miles outside Baywater. I'm stalled. Engine won't turn over and the sea—" she glanced out over the frothing waves and blistering wind "—is getting bad."

"Name of the boat?"

"*Wet Noodle*," Terry said, cringing at the ridiculous name for the rusting pile of flotsam. "If you could just call the Coast Guard for me—"

"No Coast Guard around here, ma'am," the operator said, a low country accent drawing out her words until they were a soothing lullaby of sound. Comforting, soothing. "But we'll get someone right out to help you. You just hang on a bit, all right?"

Lowering to admit, but she did need help. Soon. She should have checked the weather before setting out this morning. Should have checked out the boat, but that would have been too smart. Too logical. And she hadn't been feeling logical this morning.

She'd been feeling…*restless*.

"That's good. Thanks." She nodded, as if the operator could see her. "Could you get them to hurry, though?"

Then the voice was gone and Terry was alone again. She dumped the phone back into her purse and braced her feet wide apart, to help keep her balance as the choppy waves crashed against the rusted hull of the boat from hell.

Hang on?

What else could she do but hang on?

"One of Bucky's boats," Monk shouted, despite the mic he wore on his helmet. "The poor fool that rented it, couldn't even use the radio to call for help—didn't work—had to do it on a cell phone."

Disgusted, Aidan said, "I'm surprised any of Bucky's boats are still floating. The man's a menace."

Monk nodded. "Someone should put that old coot out of business."

"Yeah, but without Bucky renting out those rust buckets of his, who the hell would we have to rescue?"

Monk shook his head somberly. A bear of a man at six-four and about two hundred fifty pounds, Monk took up a lot of space and always managed to look as though he'd just lost his best friend. He leaned out and stared down at the ocean as it whizzed past beneath them, he said, "Things're getting ugly down there, Reilly."

Monk's voice came through the earpiece he wore, despite the thunderous noise of the Marine helicopter as it sliced through the air about twenty feet above the surface of the water.

Aidan looked out for himself and noticed the froth of whitecaps and the choppy sea. Storm was brewing out in the Atlantic and it was getting closer. Hell, he could feel the chopper pushing hard against a headwind. Another couple of days, that hurricane just might hit landfall and then they were in for a hell of a ride.

"Looks bad, man," Monk said, still shaking his head.

"Relax, Monk. You don't have to dive in, remember?"

"Damn right I remember," the big man said, glancing at him. "No way in hell do I go swimming in a fish's dining room. You divers are nuts."

"You know most people are afraid of flying."

"There's no figuring people," Monk said and pulled a stick of gum out of the pocket of his flight suit. Unwrapping it, he added, "They'll go swimming with sharks, or sit out on a puny little boat to wave to whales, but they're afraid of a plane—precision aeronautics." Shaking his head, he popped the gum into his mouth and chewed. "Makes no sense."

"Almost on 'em," J.T. said over the mic from the pilot's seat. "E.T.A. two minutes."

Monk grabbed hold of one of the chicken straps and leaned far out of the chopper, more at home in the air than most people were on land. "Yep. There it is. Hell, whoever's on it's lucky it hasn't sunk yet. Damn that Bucky to hell and back. Prob'ly a couple hungry sharks down there right now."

"Jeez, Monk," J.T. complained. "Let it go, will ya?"

Aidan laughed as he geared up, checking his dive

suit and adjusting his mask. "Just be ready with the basket. We'll bring up the passengers and leave the boat. Let Bucky worry about hauling it back in."

"Now that's justice," Monk muttered, "send the old bastard out in one of his own boats."

Aidan smiled and stepped to the open hatchway. J.T. brought the chopper in low and hovered steadily, despite the wind trying to push them back toward shore. Glancing down into the boiling surf, Aidan shot a quick look at the small boat rocking wildly with the waves, then lifted a hand to Monk, held on to his face mask and jumped.

That first second out of the chopper was the biggest rush he knew. For that one moment, he was flying. Free and easy, the wind whipping around him, tethered to neither land nor ship, and Aidan felt...*alive* in a way he never could if he were stuck in a nine to five job.

Then he hit the water and the icy slap of it jolted him just like always. Darkness grabbed at him with cold hands and held him briefly in the shadowy quiet. Then he was kicking for the surface again and breaching, just ten feet or so from the boat that looked as if it was going to rock itself to pieces any second.

Being one of Bucky's Bombs, it probably would.

He struck out with strong strokes and in a few seconds was grabbing hold of the side of the boat. Someone on board grabbed his hands and when he tipped his face up to say hello, his grin died.

"Terry?"

"For God's sake," she complained. *"You?"*

"Just what I was thinking, damn it."

Aidan shook his head, then waved to Monk, still hanging out of the chopper. In another second, the man had the rescue basket swung out into the wind and was winching it down carefully, one hand on the cable.

Turning his gaze back on Terry, Aidan hooked his arms over the side of the boat and said, "What the hell were you thinking coming out now?"

She pushed windblown hair out of her eyes and glared at him. Not much of a welcome for the guy who'd come to save her.

Her lips pinched together as if she really didn't want to answer. But she did. "I just wanted to go out on the water for a couple of hours."

"Been watching any news lately?"

"No."

"Guess not. Ever heard of Hurricane Igor?"

"Hurricane?" She shouted to be heard over the wake of the chopper.

Torn between amazement and fury at the astonishment on her features, Aidan snapped, "Get your stuff, we're taking you out of here."

"What about the boat?"

"We'll radio it in. Bucky can come get his own damn boat this time."

She stared at him. "How'd you know I rented it—"

His back teeth ground together. "It's rusty as hell

and it's dead as Moses. Has to be one of Bucky's. Now let's get going, huh?"

Terry had already turned away, though, gathering up her purse and a small thermos.

"You ready?" he shouted as the rescue basket dragged through the water toward him.

"As ready as I'll ever be."

"Swing your legs over the side." He called out and reached to steady her as she did what she was told. With one hand, he grabbed the basket, hauling it closer, then looked up at her. "You're gonna get wet."

For the first time since he'd arrived, she smiled and threw her head back, tossing her hair out of her face again. "Not as wet as I *thought* I was going to get."

Admiration roared through him like an F-18. Amazing woman. No hysterics. No whining about the situation. No fear. Just calm acceptance and simple obedience to his orders.

Aidan laughed while he held the basket steady for her. She slipped off the edge of the boat and landed inelegantly in the basket. Ocean water sloshed over the edges and surged up through the iron grillwork to soak her pale green shorts and halfway up her T-shirt. "Whoa!" she shouted as the cold gave her a solid jolt.

She held her purse aloft to keep it dry and clutched the iron railing with her free hand. Once she was in, Aidan climbed aboard, too, then waved to Monk. The winch cranked and the basket left the water, swinging wildly in the wind, turning, spinning, while Terry's grip on the rail tightened until her knuckles were white.

Aidan watched her, noted the excitement in her eyes, dusted with a healthy dose of fear, and he felt…*something*. His heart hadn't been steady since the moment he'd looked up into her green eyes. Finding her out here, in rough weather, all alone, had, for one moment, scared the tar out of him. But now, watching her take the wild ride with the enthusiasm of a kid at an amusement park, he felt something completely different.

Something deeper.

Something warmer.

Something dangerous.

By the time they reached the base, she was shivering despite the blanket Monk had provided. She didn't argue when Aidan told her he'd drive her home and she was damn quiet on the trip.

But then, so was he. Too busy trying to figure out just what he was feeling to speak, he concentrated on driving—though he indulged himself more than once with quick, sidelong glances at his passenger.

They were more than halfway home when the storm jumped into high gear. Lightning sliced the gray clouds open like a knife puncturing a water balloon and rain poured out in a blinding slash.

"Glad I'm not still on the boat," she muttered, clutching the blanket a little more tightly around her.

Her voice, quiet, was almost lost in the pounding of the rain on the roof of Aidan's SUV. He gripped the steering wheel with both fists and asked, "Why the hell were you out there at all?"

She sighed and let her head drop to the seat back. "I just wanted to be out on the ocean for a while. To just…*be*."

"And you decided to wait for hurricane weather for this outing?"

"I didn't know about the hurricane."

"Most people check the weather before they head out in a boat."

"Well, I'm not most people, I guess then, am I?"

"Already knew that," he muttered, remembering that stab of shock he'd felt when he'd seen her, sitting in that damn rust bucket. "And why the hell did you rent a boat from Bucky of all damn people?"

"He was the only one open."

He slapped one hand against the wheel and squinted into the driving rain. It was like trying to drive through a carwash. "Well, that should have told you something right there. Nobody in their right mind is renting out boats with a hurricane coming in."

"I didn't know about the hurricane. I already told you."

He blew out a breath and took one hand off the wheel long enough to scrape it across his face. "Fine. Fine. Not going to argue that one again."

"Gee, thanks." She turned her head on the seat

back to look at him. "Not that I don't appreciate the rescue, but I could do without the lecture."

"Yeah, probably." But damn it, if they hadn't been able to get to her, then what? She'd have been stranded in the middle of the damn ocean with a hurricane headed her way. In one of Bucky's boats, for God's sake. Which was about as safe as taking a cruise in a colander.

"Shook me a little, seeing you out there," he admitted finally.

"Shook me, too," she said. "Been awhile since I've been in a situation like that."

"You've done this before?" he asked, and made a left off the main highway into a subdivision of tidy homes and narrow streets. The trees lining Elmwood Drive were dancing and swaying with the punch of the wind and experience told him that if Igor didn't change directions mighty damn soon, most of those trees were going to be pulled up by the roots and tossed like sticks.

"Last time," she said, capturing his attention again, "it was on the Gulf Coast. Took a hired boat out and a friend of mine ran it across a sand bar. Ripped the bottom out and we were treading water for what felt like days."

He shook his head. Sounded like something he and his buddies would get into. Why it bothered him to think of *Terry* being in that situation, he didn't want to acknowledge.

"It's your fault anyway," she said suddenly, her tone shifting from memory to fury.

"Yeah?" He snorted an astonished laugh as he pulled into Donna's driveway. Throwing the gearshift into Park, he yanked up on the brake hard enough to spring the damn thing, then turned to face the woman beside him. "How d'you figure?"

"Last night." She waved one hand at him accusingly. "That motorcycle ride. That—" She snapped her mouth shut, shook her head, and opened the car door to a blast of wind and rain that swamped her the moment she stepped out. She slammed the door hard enough to rock the car, then stalked around the front end and headed for the porch.

Aidan was just a heartbeat behind her. Damned if he'd let her say something halfway and then stop. He joined her on the narrow porch and was grateful for the slight overhang that kept most of the punishing rain from slamming their heads. The wind pushed at them though and slanted the rain in at them sideways. Her hands were shaking. So Aidan took the key from her and opened the door.

She stepped into the foyer of Donna Fletcher's bungalow and Aidan stepped in after her, before she could close the door on him. He swung the door closed behind him, then turned to face her.

"Thanks for the ride home," she said tightly, lifting her chin in an age old gesture of defiance. "Bye."

Terry's insides were jumping. She'd been stranded

on a storm-tossed ocean, picked up in an iron basket and helicoptered to a Marine base. She'd had rain and wind and noise all before she'd had two cups of coffee.

But none of that accounted for what she was feeling at the moment. She felt as though she were balanced on the very edge of a cliff, with rocks below and no guardrail above. And it wasn't the rescue at sea doing it to her, damn it.

It was *Aidan.*

She swallowed hard, pushed past him and marched through the small, neat living room to the kitchen beyond. She hit the light switch on the wall and kept walking, straight through the bright yellow room to the service porch.

Aidan was right behind her.

She heard his heavy steps, but would have *felt* his presence even if she couldn't hear him.

She hadn't really expected him to leave, but oh, how she'd hoped he would. At the moment, her emotions were as tangled as her wind-tossed hair and spending more time with Aidan wasn't going to help any.

For heaven's sake, he'd jumped out of a helicopter to ride to her rescue. She leaned on the gleaming white washing machine, closed her eyes and she could still see him, jumping out of that chopper, hitting the water and disappearing beneath the surface. Even before she'd known it was Aidan, she'd been caught up in the...*heroics* of the diver.

Then, when she'd seen him grinning up at her, her heart had jumped in her chest. The man affected her in ways no one else ever had.

And, damn it, she didn't know what to do about that.

"Finish," Aidan said, taking hold of her arm and turning her around to face him.

She ignored the blistering sensation of heat that snaked up her arm from where his skin met hers. "Finish what?"

"What you were saying. The motorcycle—and the—" he prompted.

She inhaled sharply, blew it out and tapped the toe of her soaking wet shoe against the floor. Glancing up at him, she demanded, "You're not going to let this go, are you?"

"Nope."

Another breath. Another stall. She shifted her gaze from his to the window over the back door. Rain pelted against the glass. Though it was barely noon, it looked like dusk outside. Wind rattled the window glass and howled under the eaves of the house, sounding like lost souls looking for a way out.

Well hell. She knew just how they felt.

She needed a way out of this situation and she didn't think she was going to get one. Aidan's hand tightened on her arm.

Finally she turned to meet his gaze again. "Fine. The *kiss,* all right? Happy now?"

"Delirious."

"Good. Now go away."

"Not likely."

"Seriously, Aidan." She kept her voice steady, which was no small task, considering the way her heart was thumping in her chest, "I think you should leave."

"Probably should," he admitted, sliding his hand up her arm. "But not about to."

"This is so not a good idea," she muttered, already leaning toward him, lifting her face.

"I hear that."

"But we're going to anyway," she said and ended with a hopeful, "aren't we?"

"Oh, yeah."

Seven

Terry sighed into him as Aidan pulled her close. His arms came around her and Terry lost herself in his eyes. Blue. Deeper than the sky, wilder than the sea.

Then his mouth took hers, her own eyes closed and stars exploded behind her shuttered lids. Every square inch of her body lit up and flashed like a neon sign at midnight. Tingles of awareness skittered through her and she forgot to breathe.

But then, air was overrated anyway.

He parted her lips and her tongue tangled with his in a frenzied, twisting dance of rocketing desire. Her heartbeat ratcheted into a fierce pounding that nearly deafened her. Her blood raced, her mind went blissfully blank and she gave herself up to the incredible sensation of taking and being taken.

His hands swept up and down her back and finally settled on her behind. She felt the imprint of each of his fingers against the cold, damp fabric of her shorts and he heated her so that she wouldn't have been surprised to see steam rising up around them.

She reached for him, linking her arms around his neck and pulling him closer, tighter, to her. Mouths meshed, breath mingling, sighs humming in the air, she felt him surround her with the kind of heat she'd never known before.

This was new.

This was amazing.

This was terrifying.

One small corner of her brain remained oddly rational despite the rush of hunger leaving her dazzled and breathless. And when he pulled his mouth from hers to run his tongue down the length of her throat, Terry tipped her head back, stared at the ceiling and tried to listen to that rationality.

She knew this was a mistake. Knew that there could be nothing between her and this man. And *knew,* without a doubt, that if he stopped touching her, she'd simply dissolve into a sticky, gooey puddle of unresolved want.

A low, deep tingle started just south of the pit of her stomach. She twisted against him, rocking her hips instinctively against his, pressing close, needing…needing…

"You're killing me," Aidan whispered, his breath brushing her skin until goose bumps raced gleefully up and down her spine.

"Trust me," she managed to say, "I don't want you *dead*."

He chuckled and she felt the low vibration of his laughter move through his body. Her hands swept across his back, tracing muscles barely hidden beneath the soft fabric of his T-shirt. And oh, she wanted his skin beneath her hands. She wanted to define every inch of his sculpted chest and back with her fingertips. She wanted to trail her hands down his body slowly, watching his eyes flash and spark as she took his length in her hands.

"Oh, boy," she whispered brokenly as her own thoughts fired her need to a fever pitch that left her nearly breathless.

"Yeah," he murmured, nibbling at the base of her throat, "just what I was thinking. Need to touch you."

"Oh, yeah. Now. Please now," she said, shutting down that small rational voice in her head. She didn't want reason. She didn't want to think.

She wanted an orgasm, damn it.

His hands moved, sliding between their bodies to the waistband of her shorts. Her breath came fast and furious as she felt him fumble with the button and zipper. Silently she cried, *Now, now, now. Hurry, hurry, hurry.*

She was so close.

It had been so long.

Too long since she'd felt a man's hands on her.

And even then, it hadn't been like this.

It had *never* been like this.

Terry fought for air. Fought to stand still. Fought to not knock his hands out of the way and undo her shorts herself.

Finally, *finally,* she felt the button give and the zipper slide down and she groaned as he slid one hand across her abdomen. "Aidan…"

"Have to touch you, Terry. Have to feel your heat. Now. Now."

"Now," she agreed and kept a tight grip on his shoulders as his hand slipped beneath the elastic band of her silk and lace panties and down, further, further until his fingertips touched her core and she jolted in his arms. "Aidan!"

He bit her neck gently, lightly, then stroked her skin with his tongue as his fingers worked their magic. He dipped first one finger and then two into her depths and she rocked against him, wanting more, wanting to feel him deeper, wanting to feel a *different* part of him, full and deep within her body.

She shifted her position, widening her stance, welcoming him higher, closer, and still it wasn't enough.

"Oh…my…*Aidan…*"

"More," he murmured and before she knew what was happening, he'd pulled his hand free, then tugged her shorts and panties down and off. Grabbing her at the waist, he lifted her, then plopped her down onto the washing machine.

The cold metal bit into her skin, but nothing could stop the flames consuming her. Terry didn't think about what they were doing. Didn't stop to care that he was still dressed while she was mostly naked on her friend's service porch.

The rain hammered at the roof and windows. The wind shrieked and slammed into the house. It was as if even nature had been pushed farther than it could take and had been forced to surrender itself to the moment.

Terry ran her hands over his face, smoothing her thumbs over his mouth, his cheekbones. Her vision was blurred with want. Her breathing staggered in and out of her lungs.

He leaned in and kissed her hungrily, desperately, grinding his mouth against hers in a fierce assault that left her trembling and starving for more. But he pulled away, despite her clinging hands, despite her soft moans of protest.

His big, strong hands grabbed her hips and pulled her close to the edge of the steel machine and then he parted her thighs, pushing her legs apart with gentle determination.

"Aidan…" she whispered and heard the plea in her

own voice and couldn't be embarrassed by it. She was too far gone. Too far along the road of no return. She knew only need. Knew only the hunger that had her in its grasp and wouldn't let go. "Touch me."

He cupped her cheek in the palm of one hand, bent to kiss her briefly, then moved back to stare into her eyes while he dipped his fingers into her heat again. In and out, his fingers built a rhythm that she felt right down to her bones.

"I've never wanted *anyone* the way I want you. Never."

She laughed. Shortly, harshly, desperately. "Then take me, already."

He grinned and that dimple of his shot a flame of something sweet and sharp into her heart. Grabbing her hips with both hands again, he dropped to one knee in front of her and Terry's breath stopped. She knew what he was going to do. Knew it, felt it and wanted it with a passion more fierce than anything she'd ever felt before.

His strong hands gripped her hips, holding her in place. Her heart stopped—hell, the *world* stopped— as she watched him lean in to take her in the most intimate way possible.

His mouth covered her and she groaned aloud, rocking into him. Leaning back, she braced her hands on the washing machine, searching for purchase in a suddenly spinning universe. But Aidan's hands on her hips kept her centered even when she felt herself falling, falling, into a chasm filled with spikes of pleasure and whirlpools of almost delirious need.

He tasted her, his tongue stroking, licking, tasting. His breath dusted her heat, pumping her even higher, faster. Again and again, he dipped into her center, his tongue defining every line, every curve, every inner most secret.

And Terry watched him, unable to look away. Unable to take her gaze from him. Her body rocked in his grasp as she rode the crest of a wave that had been too long banked inside her. She felt herself spiraling, flying faster. A blissful sort of tension gripped her and tightened almost painfully. Her goal was close, and getting closer with every passing second.

She lifted one hand and cupped the back of his head. His short, black hair felt soft beneath her palm. His tongue stroked her core again, in a long, stroking caress that sent her rushing forward toward the fireworks she knew were waiting.

"Aidan!" She shouted his name as the first spasm shattered what was left of her control. Holding him tightly to her, she concentrated solely on the feel of him so intimately joined to her. Her body trembled, her heart ached.

And when the fireworks finally exploded within, she called his name again.

This time in a broken whisper.

When the last of her climax had passed, Aidan stood up and pulled her into the circle of his arms.

She melted into him, locking her legs around his middle and drawing him in close.

She staggered him.

His own heart pounded in tandem with hers. He'd felt her release in every cell of his body. He'd felt the joy, experienced the pleasure and shared the hunger.

And now he wanted more.

Sweeping his hands up, he bracketed her face in his palms and stared into eyes gone glassy with unleashed passion.

"Aidan," she said, struggling to catch her breath, "that was…"

"…just a warm-up," he finished for her and kissed her, swallowing her sigh. Her arms came around him and she scooted closer to him on the stupid washing machine. "I want you," he said when he could manage to tear himself off her mouth. "I want you really bad."

"I'm so glad," she said, giving him a quick smile that shattered something inside him. She leaned in to kiss him again, then stopped, holding him at arm's length as she looked deeply into his eyes. "But what about the bet?"

The bet.

Aidan's already fogged over brain started clicking. If he gave in to what he wanted, he'd lose that stupid bet and end up in a grass skirt and a coconut bra. And what was worse, he'd have to listen to his brothers ragging on him the way he'd been hassling *them* for the last few weeks.

He looked at Terry. Felt the slim strength of her legs locked around his hips. Noted the full, luscious lips just a breath away from his.

Didn't take long to make up his mind.

"Screw the bet."

"I was so hoping you'd say that," Terry whispered, and dropped her hands to the waistband of his jeans.

The backs of her fingers brushed against his abdomen and Aidan's body tightened even further. If he didn't have her soon, he was a dead man. And he wouldn't be dying happy.

"Right there with you, babe," he muttered, dropping a kiss on the top of her head, the curve of her shoulder. "This is crazy."

"Oh, yeah, no doubt.

"And *so* necessary," she whispered on a choked off laugh.

"Right again. Love a woman who's right so often."

"Unusual man," she murmured as she finally worked the last button of his fly free.

"I like to think so," he managed to say through clenched teeth.

"No underwear," she whispered, sliding her hand down, down, *bingo*.

"Too confining." He hissed in another breath as she stroked him.

"So are your jeans."

"Good point." He let go of her long enough to shove at his jeans—and his cell phone rang. "Damn it."

"Don't answer it," she urged, scraping her palms up now, under his shirt, across his chest.

"Have to. I'm on call," he muttered grimly, already digging for the damn thing out of his jeans pocket. He flipped it open, checked the number and cursed again, viciously. He glanced at her. "It's the base."

Stepping away from her reluctantly, he answered it. "What?"

"Hey, boy, we got another call. Get your ass back here."

J.T.'s voice sounded almost cheerful—for that alone, Aidan wanted to wring his neck. Shoving one hand through his hair, he muttered, "What's up?"

"Some guy fell off a charter fishing boat. Nobody noticed till they got back to the dock." J.T. snorted. "Apparently the guy was a real idiot and people were so grateful that he was 'quiet,' they never questioned it."

"Who the hell would go fishing in this weather?"

"Got enough money to convince the captain, a charter boat's gonna give it a go. You coming or what?"

"Yeah. Be there in fifteen." Aidan flipped the phone closed, heaved a sigh and buttoned up his jeans. Then bending down, he grabbed Terry's shorts and tossed them to her.

"You're leaving."

"Have to."

"So," she said, giving him a smile he knew she wasn't feeling. "I'm not the only idiot out on the water today."

"Looks that way." He watched her and everything in him wanted to ignore the call to duty. For the first time…*ever,* he wanted to blow it all off. To stay here. To lose himself in a woman he'd known less than a week.

That shocked the hell out of him.

He scraped one hand across his face, shoved the phone back into his pocket and stepped up close to her, still perched on the edge of the washing machine. A buzz of passion, excitement, still coursed through him. He reached out and took her face between his palms. Kissing her once, twice, he pulled back and looked into her eyes for a long minute before speaking again.

"Do me a favor?"

She licked her lips and sent a white-hot blast of need shooting right through him.

"What?"

Aidan inhaled slowly, deeply, and let the air slide from his lungs. "Stay home today. Keep the shop closed."

"Aidan, I—"

"Trust me," he interrupted neatly. "Nobody's going to be out shopping today. They'll all be hunkering down, waiting for the hurricane."

She sighed. "If the hurricane *is* coming, then I need to go to the shop. Board up the windows. Donna told me where everything is and—"

"I'll do it."

She bristled. "I'm not helpless, Aidan. I can do it."

"Didn't say you were helpless," he muttered, wondering where the soft buzz of sexual electricity had gone. "Just—*wait* for me, all right? I'll help when I'm off-duty. You want to start boarding up here, okay by me. Just watch yourself."

For a second or two, he thought she might argue. Then she nodded.

"I will."

He kissed her again, one last, lingering kiss filled with promise and disappointment and regret. Then he took a step back and turned for the doorway to the kitchen. "Gotta go."

"Aidan?"

He stopped to look at her.

"Be careful out there."

A slow, wicked smile curved his mouth. "I'm *always* careful, babe."

And then he was gone.

Eight

The neighbors helped.

It seemed when hurricane season rolled around, there were *no* strangers.

Rain slashed at Baywater, coming in so fast and so furiously that it was hard to see as far as across the street. The wind whipped through the trees and tore loose shingles off houses that shuddered with the force of the pre-hurricane gusts.

Donna had been prepared, Terry gave her friend points for that. All of the wood used for boarding up the windows and glass topped doors was stacked neatly in the garage and clearly labeled, telling Terry exactly where each piece went. With the help of a couple of neighbors, Donna's house was as protected as it was going to get in just a couple of hours.

Then there was nothing to do but wait.

Making herself a cup of coffee, Terry winced as she listened to the slam of hammering rain crashing against the house. She kept the TV on, as one of Donna's neighbors had warned her to listen for evacuation notices.

Her stomach churned and her nerves were stretched to the breaking point. She cradled the coffee cup between her palms and tried not to notice the howl and shriek of the wind as it whipped past the house.

"Okay, adventure is one thing," she muttered, glancing at the ceiling as though she would be able to look through it to the storm-tossed sky above. "This is nuts."

And Aidan was out in it.

It had been hours since he'd left her to go on another rescue mission. Hours since she'd taken an easy breath. She shouldn't be worried. This was what he did. The man was trained. And good at his job. She'd seen that for herself only that morning. Though listening to the weather now, she still couldn't believe she'd been dumb enough to go out on a boat today.

But it didn't seem to matter that she knew Aidan was well trained and very capable. She felt a cold, tight fist close around her heart as her mind drew images of him leaping out of that helicopter into the churning mass of the sea. She pictured him swimming toward that lost fisherman and getting swallowed by an ocean that was determined to not give up its prize.

As those images and more raced through her brain, Terry shivered, set the coffee cup down on the kitchen counter and walked out of the room. She crossed the living room, dark now, despite the lamps turned on to keep the shadows at bay. With the boarded up windows, she felt as though she were in a coffin.

Alone.

Afraid.

Shaking her head, she grabbed the doorknob, gave it a turn and opened the door. Instantly wind whipped rain slashed at her, sweeping through the screen door into the foyer as if it had been perched on the porch, just waiting for its chance.

The world was wild.

Trees bobbed and swayed, like desperate sinners, pleading for forgiveness. Rain sluiced out of a gunmetal-gray sky. Houses were boarded up. No one was on the street. People were locked up, shut in and praying that the heaviest part of the storm would pass them by.

Terry walked to the edge of the porch, dipping her head into the wind, forcing herself forward, though it was like trying to run in a swimming pool. Her fingers curled over the rail at the edge of the porch and she squinted into the rain still slashing at her.

Stupid. She should be inside. Warm. Dry.

But inside, she was too alone. Inside, she was reminded that she was a woman apart from the rest of this tiny town at the edge of a storm. Everyone else was with their families. With people they loved or cared about.

Terry had no one.

She'd wanted it that way, of course. For years, she'd done everything she could to keep her distance from anyone or anything that might claim an attachment. She'd loved once and she'd lost and promised herself then that she wouldn't risk that kind of pain again.

Well, it had worked, she told herself now, clinging to the porch railing and watching a watery world of roaring noise and vicious winds. She'd successfully isolated herself.

And she'd never felt more alone.

The family was safe.

Aidan steered his car cautiously down the street, windshield wipers doing their best to keep up with a steady downpour, he looked at the world through a veil of water. Images were blurred, wind whipped, but his mind was clear. Focused.

He'd checked on the rest of the Reilly's. His mom was with Tina and Brian, helping Tina's nana get her house ready. And Connor and Emma were at the church, helping Liam's parishioners batten down the hatches at Saint Sebastian's.

Which left Aidan free to do what his heart was telling him to do.

Go to Terry.

After getting back to base, with a very wet, very angry fisherman, sputtering about lawsuits, he'd headed straight to the Frog House bookstore. With the help of the other local businessmen, he'd managed to board up Donna's place and help Selma tie her shop down as well. Now, they'd done all they could and all they could do was wait.

And there was nowhere he'd rather wait than with Terry.

She'd been there, in the back of his mind, all day. Throughout the rescue calls, throughout all the hurricane preparations, she'd been there, lurking in the shadows of his mind. Reminding him that he had more now to think about than himself. More to take care of than his family.

"Which was damned weird when you think about it," he muttered, steering his SUV around a downed tree and cautiously inching forward, on the lookout for fallen electrical wires.

He hadn't *asked* to care about anyone.

Hadn't *wanted* to be worried about a curvy blonde with a smart mouth.

And yet…instead of hanging around the base as he would have normally—in case they were called out again—he was driving through hell just so he could see her. Reassure himself that she was all right. He'd tried calling her, but the phone lines were down. No surprise. They were usually the first to go in a big storm.

But this was the first time in memory that not being able to make a phone call had turned his insides to jelly.

His fists tightened around the steering wheel as the car was buffeted by wind. He bent his head to look up through the windshield and winced as he watched trees leaning precariously over the street, shimmying as leaves were whipped free, sailing through the air like tiny green missiles.

Aidan made the turn on Elmwood and barely noticed the boarded-up houses and the abandoned look of the normally cozy, kid-filled street.

His gaze locked on one house. He headed toward it as if drawn by a powerful force he had no intention of fighting.

Then he saw her.

Standing on the porch, clutching the railing that shuddered in the wind as if it were a lifeline. His heart thundered in his chest as he watched her blond hair whipping around her head. She lifted one hand to shield her eyes as he got closer and he saw the brief flash of welcome dart across her features as he pulled into the driveway.

He drove as close to the garage as he could, where the car would be protected on one side at least, by the house itself. Then he parked, shut off the engine, set the brake and opened the door.

The wind grabbed it from him, wrenching it wildly out of his grasp and he had to fight to get it closed again.

Once he had, he bolted for the house, long legs striding through the mud and standing water, rain pounding him, wind pushing at him, as if deliberately trying to keep him from her.

But nothing could.

He hit the porch, grabbed Terry and pulled her into the house. When the door was closed and locked behind them, he pulled her into his arms and simply held her, enjoying the feel of her cold, wet body plastered against his.

"What were you doing out there?"

"I couldn't stand it in here anymore," she admitted, holding on to him with a grip as strong as his own. "It felt so...*empty* in here. So quiet."

He laughed shortly and lifted his head, hearing the wind, the rain and the low-pitched voice of the weatherman on the television. *"Quiet?"*

She looked up at him and blew out a long breath. "I felt...alone. And I couldn't take it anymore."

"You're not alone now," he pointed out.

"No." She smiled. "And boy am I glad to see you."

He shifted one hand to touch her cheek, sliding his fingertips across her smooth, pale skin. "Same here."

Her hands moved, from his back to his front, skimming up the front of his now soaking wet T-shirt. Yet, he felt the heat of her touch right down to his bones.

"You were gone a long time."

He sucked in air. "The lost fisherman wasn't easy to find."

"But you did."

"Yeah." He slid one hand along her spine, noted her shiver and moved his hand lower, lower, until he could caress the curve of her behind. His gaze searched hers, for what, he wasn't sure. "J.T. flew all over the damn place. Monk and I were hanging out the hatch and Monk spotted the guy's orange vest."

She inhaled sharply as his hand on her behind pulled her tight against him. Licking her lips, she closed her eyes briefly and whispered, "So he's okay?"

"Yeah. Ungrateful bastard, though." Aidan smiled. "Already talking about suing the charter boat captain and maybe *us*."

"For what?" she asked, clearly stunned.

"He wrenched his neck climbing into the rescue basket."

"Idiot."

"That about covers it." He moved his hand again, this time to the waistband of her shorts. Then he dipped beneath the fabric and scraped his palm over her damp, chilled skin. He sucked in air. "You didn't put your underwear back on?"

She shook her head and closed her eyes again as his fingers kneaded the soft flesh of her behind. "Forgot about it. Got busy…ohhh…"

"You're killing me again."

She smiled lazily. "I don't think so."

He cupped the back of her head with his free hand and threading his fingers through her hair, tipped her face up to his. He bent and gave her a kiss. And another. "I have a feeling this is going somewhere."

"Feels like it to me, too," she managed to say and then swallowed hard.

"So before we get started, you should know I already boarded up the store."

"Oh, good. Thank you."

He grinned quickly. "No arguments? No *'you should have taken me with you'?*"

"Nope," she murmured.

The wind howled again, and the front door rattled loudly as if trying to hold its own against a ravening beast fighting to gain entry.

"We're trapped here, you know. Can't leave in this."

She opened her eyes and looked up at him. "Who wants to leave?"

"Not me, babe."

"You've got to stop calling me 'babe.'"

He grinned again. "I'll work on it. Later."

"Oh, yeah. *Later.*"

Swooping in, he took her mouth with his and showed her just how much he wanted her. How much he'd been thinking of her. How thoughts of her had been haunting him throughout the day.

She opened her mouth to his and when her tongue met his, Aidan sucked in air like a dying man hoping for just another minute or two of life. He tasted her, explored every inch of her warmth, drawing her heat into himself and holding it close, letting it feed the fires licking at his insides.

This.

This is what had kept him going through the long, hard day. The promise of touching her, exploring her, having her beneath him, over him.

His hand on her butt tightened, squeezing, and she moaned into his mouth, squirming closer to him, brushing her hardened nipples against his chest until Aidan was sure she'd left an imprint on his skin right through his shirt.

"Flat surface," he muttered, tearing his mouth from hers.

"Now," she agreed and stepped out of his embrace. Taking his hand, she led him on a quick march through the living room to the hallway and the bedrooms beyond.

Aidan had been in Donna's house before. He knew the layout and he knew when Terry made a right turn, they were headed for the master bedroom. He grabbed her up, unwilling to wait another moment before touching her, feeling her.

She yelped in surprise, then settled against him, running her hands beneath the collar of his T-shirt, splaying her palms against his shoulders, his back. Heat. Incredible heat, speared through him, nearly stopping him in his tracks.

He dropped his head to hers and kissed her again, hungrily, desperately, a man on the edge and ready to jump feetfirst into the abyss.

Then they were in the bedroom and Terry leaned down from her perch in his arms to grab the edge of the handmade quilt covering the mattress and toss it to the foot of the bed. Lacy pillowcases covered the plump pillows and fresh white sheets looked like heaven, even in the gloom.

With the windows boarded up, the room was like a cave, dimly lit, sheltered, tucked away from the storm-tossed world outside.

An island of seclusion.

"Turn on a light," he murmured, swinging her down onto her own two feet. "I want to see you."

A long breath shuddered into her lungs, but she nodded as she crossed the room to turn on a small desk light covered by a Tiffany style lampshade. Pale, ghostly colors danced suddenly around the room, gleaming through the stained-glass shade.

Terry just stared at him. There was no turning back now. And maybe there never had been. Maybe they'd been destined to reach this moment from the instant they'd met. Hadn't she been drawn to him, in spite of her best efforts? Hadn't she felt the magic of his touch in quick, near electrical jolts of awareness every time he was near?

Hadn't she spent the last several hours remembering that incredible orgasm he'd given her and wanting *more?*

While he watched her, she took another steadying breath and quietly, soundlessly, lifted the hem of her dark green shirt up and over her head. He sucked in a breath and she felt his hungry gaze fasten on her breasts, still hidden from him behind their shield of lace.

Slowly, teasingly, daringly, she lifted her hands to the front closure and snapped it open. Then she shrugged out of the lacy fabric and let it fall to the floor behind her.

"Terry…"

She threw her shoulders back and with his gaze locked on her every move, slowly undid the button and zipper of her wet shorts. Then she let them go and they slid down her legs to puddle at her feet.

"If I don't have you in the next couple of minutes," he said, his voice a rumble of sound lower, more demanding and insistent than the thunder outside, "I swear I'm a dead man."

She smiled, feeling a rush of feminine power swamp her, rushing through her blood, making her limbs tremble and her brain shut down. "You're wearing too many clothes again."

He gave her a quick smile that sent a bolt of something delicious straight down to the core of her.

"Guess I am." In seconds, he'd peeled off his shirt, unhooked his jeans and shucked them and his shoes and socks. He let her look her fill, just as he had.

And Terry wanted to *whistle*.

She'd never seen a more gorgeous man in her life. Every inch of him was tanned to a golden-brown and every muscle rippling across his arms and chest and abdomen were sharply defined. And as for the rest of him, his…

"Oh, my."

He grinned and stalked toward her, grabbing her tightly to him, pressing her naked body along the length of his. Hard to soft, heat to heat. She felt the hard, jutting strength of him poking at her and everything inside her went to damp neediness. Her breasts crushed against his chest, her nipples tingled in anticipation even as he took her mouth with his, tangling his tongue with her, tasting, taking, giving.

Her mind whirled.

Her blood raced.

Her body quickened as it had only hours ago, only this time, it was more. More, because she'd had a part of him and wanted all of him.

"Fill me," she murmured, breaking the kiss and nibbling at his neck. "Fill me completely."

Thunder rolled, rain pounded and the wind groaned. The house shimmied, boarded windows rattled and the world seemed to take a breath.

Then he lifted her, as if she weighed nothing. Two big hands at her hips and she was airborne, clutching at his shoulders for balance, looking down into his hungry eyes. She read the passion, the untamed fury and felt a matching need rise in her. His strength cradled her as he lowered her slowly onto the hardened length of him.

"Aidan..." she whispered his name as he entered her, pushing into her depths with a steady determination. Her damp heat welcomed him, and her body adjusted, making room, taking him deeper.

She locked her legs around his middle and leaned back, trusting his strength, letting her head fall and her hair swing wild and wet from her head in a dripping blond curtain.

"Deeper," she crooned, using her legs, hooked over his hips, to pull him closer. "*Deeper*, Aidan. I need to feel *all* of you."

An inferno of need rose up around them, trapping them, drawing them both deeper into the gaping canyon of desire.

He dipped his head to take one of her nipples into his mouth and as his lips and tongue and teeth worked the sensitive tip, a moan slipped from Terry that left her whimpering in its wake.

Every inch of her felt alive, tingling, *desperate*. When he suckled her, she felt the drawing power of him clear to her toes and still, it wasn't *enough*.

Aidan heard that moan and it triggered something inside him that pushed him over the brink of control into the whirlwind of passion. He'd never known need so fierce, so all consuming.

Never tasted passion tinged with desperation.

Never felt anything like this woman he held so intimately.

He tightened his grip on her hips and pulled her down harder onto his length, pushing the whole of him into her depths, savoring the feel of being surrounded by her heat. Lifting his head, he took pleasure in watching the play of emotions on her face. Watching her teeth bite into her full bottom lip. Hearing the whispered breaths and edgy sighs.

Arms straining, muscles screaming, he used every ounce of his strength to set a rhythm designed to drive them both wild. He watched the play of emerald, green and gold light dazzle her pale, creamy skin and lost himself in the wonder of the moment. Her fingernails dug into his shoulders and she lifted her hips in his grasp and then lowered herself onto him again, grinding her body against his as if she couldn't take him deep enough. Hold him tight enough.

His brain short-circuited.

His heart hammered in his chest.

His mouth went dry and his vision blurred until Terry was his whole world. The universe, wrapped up in pale, jewel toned light, sighing, writhing, moaning.

"It's…coming…Aidan…" Whispered, broken words, trembling from her lips as she twisted on him, like a live butterfly on a pin.

"Let it come, Terry," he murmured, tightening his grasp on her hips, plunging himself deeper, higher, inside her. "There'll be another one. Let this one come."

She lifted her head and looked at him through glassy eyes. "Come with me," she ordered, licking her lips, breath coming in short, hard gasps.

Then linking one arm around his neck, she stretched out her other hand, reached beneath the spot where their bodies joined and cupped him, her fingers exploring, rubbing, stroking.

Lights exploded behind his eyes.

Aidan held her tight.

He heard her groan.

Felt her body implode.

And finally allowed his to follow.

Nine

Outside, Mother Nature shrieked.

Inside, Mother Nature celebrated.

Even before the last of the tremors had eased from him, Aidan wanted Terry again, with, if possible, a deeper need than before.

He'd never experienced anything like this. Never known need that couldn't be satisfied, desire that couldn't be quenched. Even now, still buried inside her, his body stirred, eager for another bout. Another surging race through madness to completion.

"That was—" Terry's head dropped to his shoulder *"—amazing."*

He smiled into her wet hair, kissed her head and murmured, "And I don't do my best work standing up."

"Could've fooled me." She lifted her head to look at him. Their gazes locked and he watched as new hunger lit up in her eyes, chasing away the shadows that had first intrigued him.

She moved on him, lifting her hips slightly, only to lower herself again and his body reacted in a heartbeat.

"Again?" she whispered, nibbling at his neck, tonguing his skin, leaving a damp, warm trail against already fevered flesh.

"And again and again," Aidan promised, already moving toward the bed.

One part of his tortured brain heard the howl and cry of the wind, the hammering of the rain. But he paid no attention.

They were warm.

They were safe.

They were stranded.

Here.

Together.

That was enough.

He pulled free of her body long enough to lay her down on the crisp white sheets that smelled of lavender. He'd only uncoupled from her so that he could feel the rush of entering her again. Otherwise, he would have been happy to stay locked within her depths for the rest of eternity.

She moved on the bed, scooting back, sliding her feet on the sheets until her knees lifted and her thighs parted. He looked his fill of her and knew it would never be enough. Reaching out, he touched her center, smoothing his fingertips over swollen, damp flesh, and watched her eyes—those incredible grass-green eyes—glaze over in a mindless daze.

"Aidan…I want you again. Now."

His heart quickened, drumming so loudly in his chest as to be deafening. Every nerve ending in his body sizzled in eager enthusiasm. But this time, he was in no rush. This time, he wanted to draw the experience out—for both of them.

He slipped first one finger and then two inside her, playing with her, stroking her, exploring her. And he watched her move against him, lifting her hips, rocking into his hand while her own hands fisted on the sheet beneath her. Her head tossed from side to side. She licked dry lips and whispered broken, half-hearted pleas as he continued to stroke her body into a firestorm of *need*.

And with every stroke of his fingers, his own body tightened until he felt rock-hard and aching for want of her. Seconds ticked past, and Aidan realized he wouldn't be able to draw this time out much longer than he had the first. Not when need crouched in his chest and hammered at him to bury himself inside her. Not when hunger roared through him and danced on each of her sighs.

Levering himself over her, he slid his hands up, up, her body, over her curves, defining every line of her with fingertips careful as he would be while caressing fragile shards of crystal.

Her back bowed as she arched into him and he dipped his head to taste her. He took first one pebbled nipple and then the other into his mouth, rolling his tongue across them, nibbling with the edges of his teeth. She lifted small hands and cupped the back of his head, holding him to her as he gently tormented her.

"Feels so good," she whispered in a harshly strained voice.

"Tastes even better," he assured her, smiling against her body as he suckled her, pulling on her flesh, trying to draw her essence inside him.

"Aidan!"

His name in a quiet cry of nerves, stretched tight, shuddered through him and he moved to cover her. To push himself home, deep within her. He knelt between her legs and as she parted her thighs in welcome and held her arms wide to draw him in, he slid into her heat again.

Diving deep, he drove himself home with a hunger that grabbed him by the throat and wouldn't let go. He rocked wildly, furiously, in and out of her body, loving the slow slide to heaven enough to put up with having to leave her with every stroke.

She moved with him, instinctively following his rhythm, then setting one of her own. Hands fisted, breaths mingled, sighs twisted in the still, jewel-colored air. She took him, all of him, and held him deeply.

He looked into her eyes and felt himself falling into their depths and knew he didn't want to save himself. Everything he wanted, needed, was right here. In this bed in the middle of a storm that was tearing at the city.

But he wanted to see her, too, so he rolled onto his back, taking her with him, astride him.

She straddled him in the soft light and smiled down at him as she continued the rhythm he'd set, moving, rocking her hips, swiveling her body against his.

She rode him with a quiet power and a tender fury. Flesh slapped against flesh. Heat burrowed into heat. He lifted his hands, covered her breasts with his palms and sucked in a frantic gulp of air when she covered his hands with her own.

Terry looked down at him and felt herself drowning in eyes the color of a stormy sea. She felt the build in her body, knew a climax was shuddering close and felt the rush of expectation tingle through her.

He pulled his hands out from under hers and let them slide down her body, fingertips dancing fluidly over her skin until she could have sworn she felt him touching her on the *inside*.

She kept her hands on her own breasts, squeezing, tweaking her nipples, tugging at them, while he watched her and his eyes went gray and cloudy. A fierce smile curved her mouth as she rocked her hips against him, taking him in as deeply as she could.

Then he dropped one hand to the spot where their bodies joined and touched the very core of her. That one supersensitive nubbin of flesh. He stroked her, once, twice—and her body exploded into a showery storm of brightly colored lights. Her head fell back as she screamed his name into the fury of the storm.

Then he flipped her onto her back and before the last trembling shiver coursed through her body, he'd claimed his own release, whispering her name just before collapsing on top of her.

What could have been minutes—or hours—later, Aidan turned his head on the pillow and looked at the woman lying beside him. In the dim light, she looked like something mystical. Something not quite of this world.

Even as he thought it, he smiled to himself, silently acknowledging that the Irish in him was coming out. With her fair hair and pale, smooth skin, she looked as though she'd been carved from alabaster by a talented, generous sculptor.

But she was real—as he was here to testify.

She turned her head on the pillow and her gaze met his. She smiled. "Well, I guess you've really lost that bet now."

He winced, but couldn't bring himself to mind very much. "Guess you could say that. Man, my brothers will never let me hear the end of this."

She rolled to her side and went up on one elbow to look at him. "Why'd you do it? Why'd you throw away the bet when you were so close to winning?"

He thought about that for a moment. Didn't have to spend much time thinking about it now, as he'd done plenty of thinking about it earlier today. In fact, *all* of today, when he'd been away from her. When he'd had just a small taste of her and was still—as he was now—eager for another. Rolling to his right side, he, too, propped himself up on one elbow and watched her as he reached out to stroke a single fingertip across the tops of her breasts.

She hissed in a breath and sighed it out.

"Because," he said, still shaken by the knowledge, "I wanted *you* more than I wanted to *win.*"

"I think that's a compliment."

"Damn straight," he said. "Believe me."

She caught his hand in hers and folded their fingers together. "Why did you want to win that silly bet so badly anyway?"

"To be the best," he answered, without hesitation. "To be the last Reilly standing."

"And now?"

He grinned. "Well, now…Liam will get the ten thousand bucks and he can start getting that new roof for the church." He paused and listened to the still screaming wind and the battering fists of rain. "And judging by this storm, he's going to need a new one. Soon."

"That's good, isn't it?"

"Sure it's good. Hell, I was going to give him the money anyway," he admitted, and realized that she was the only person he'd confessed that small truth to. And he wondered why it was he felt comfortable talking to Terry about his life—his family—everything that was important to him. Then he pushed that question to the back of his mind to be examined later. Much later. "I just wanted to *win*."

"Important, is it?"

"In *my* family? Yeah."

"But you gave it up." She rubbed the edge of her thumbnail against his palm and it was his turn to hiss in a breath.

"And I would again," he assured her.

"For an afternoon like this one," she said, "so would I."

"Glad to hear it."

She laughed, a low, throaty chuckle that set up a reaction that swept through him, carrying new heat, new need.

"Please," she said. "I'm sure you know just what a good time I had today."

"Day's not over."

"Glad to hear *that*," she said and inched a little closer to him. Tipping her head back, she confessed, "Today has been…special, I guess is the right word. I haven't been with anyone in a long time."

He'd guessed that, but he was damn happy to hear it said aloud. He didn't want to think about Terry with anyone else. Also didn't want to think that in a couple of weeks she'd be gone from his life.

So he smiled. "Well, it's been awhile for me, too."

"Poor baby."

"Sarcasm from a naked woman. I like it."

He shifted position, rolling her onto her back and dipping his head to kiss her middle. His tongue dipped in and out of her belly button and slid lower.

She combed her fingers through his short hair, her long nails gently scraping against his skull.

"The reason I told you that it had been a long time for me was that I wanted you to know that I'm not usually this kind of woman."

"What kind is that?"

"You know," she said, sighing as his breath dusted her skin and his tongue swept warm, damp caresses across her abdomen. "The fling type. I'm…more complicated than that." She paused. "Although, after today, you might not believe it."

He laughed against her flat belly. "Babe, believe me, I already knew you were complicated. But thanks for the warning."

Thunder crackled overhead and the wind slammed against the board covered windows. Terry jerked beneath Aidan and he used his hands and mouth to soothe her.

After a minute or two, she started talking again. "There've only been three men in my life. One I loved…one I thought I loved, which is pretty much the same thing." She paused. "And then there's you."

He stilled, even his heartbeat went soft and quiet. Outside, the storm blasted at the windows and doors, searching for a way in. But here in this room, another storm raged. This one in Aidan's heart. Love? Who'd said anything about love?

She laughed. "Don't look so panicked, Aidan. I wasn't proposing."

He gave her a smile he didn't feel.

"I'm just saying," she continued, pushing pillows beneath her head so she could see him clearly, "That this...*means* something to me."

He lifted his head to meet her gaze. And in all honesty, he could say, "It means something to me, too. I don't know what, Terry. Can't tell you that. But it means *something*."

"Thanks."

"For what?"

"For not trying to lie your way out of a tricky situation. For not pretending to be the love of my life. For respecting me enough to give me the truth."

"I'll always give you that, babe."

She smiled. "You know, it's interesting. I'm starting to like hearing you call me that."

"Happy to oblige." He kissed her belly again and moved a little lower.

She sighed. "I'm not looking for love anyway, Aidan. Not again."

That caught his attention. The sorrow, the pain in her voice and he knew that if he looked into her eyes, he'd see those shadows again. The ones that had haunted him from the moment they met.

And he couldn't help himself.

He looked.

Saw the pain and ached for her.

"Who was he?"

She sighed again and this simple release of pent-up breath rattled him right down to his soul.

"His name was Eric."

Aidan hated him already. No doubt tall, muscle-bound and too stupid to know what he'd had when he'd had it. "What happened to him?"

She closed her eyes. "He died."

Damn. Empathy welled up inside him. "God, Terry. I'm sorry."

"It was a long time ago."

"How long?" he wondered, because the shadows in her eyes looked fresh enough to have been born the day before. The pain was obviously still sharp.

She glanced at him and ran her fingertips along the side of his face. "Twelve years."

He blinked. She couldn't be more than thirty now. "You were a kid."

"Not for long." She moved beneath him, arching her body up to his as if to remind him that he'd been kissing her a minute or two ago and she wouldn't mind having him start back up. "I don't want to talk about it now, okay?"

"Sure. Okay," he said, mind spinning, even while his body urged him back to the business at hand.

He dipped his head again, trailing his lips and

tongue across her belly, lower, lower, until just above the triangle of soft blond curls, he noticed the thin sliver of an old scar.

He ran his finger across the faint, silvery line and kept his voice even, as he asked a question he was pretty sure he already knew the answer to. "What's this?"

She closed her eyes, let her hand fall from his head and said, "I had an operation."

"Yeah I get that. What kind?"

She blew out a breath. "Caesarean section."

"You had a baby."

"Yes."

"When you were a kid."

"Yes."

"Eric," he said, feeling his heart sink for her.

"Yes. Eric. My son." Terry's eyes filled with tears and she blinked frantically, trying to keep them at bay. Stupid. She shouldn't have started talking. Opening up a conversation that would inevitably lead them down this path.

"What happened?" Aidan asked and a part of her was surprised that she could hear his soft, low-pitched voice at all, over the freight train of sound just outside the house.

Staring up at the ceiling, she concentrated on the colored shadows tossed from the stained-glass lamp. "Why do you want to know?"

He slid back up the length of her body, flesh

brushing against flesh, hard to soft, warmth to warmth and she was so damned grateful for that *connection,* her eyes filled again. It had been a long time since she'd felt connected to anyone. And that she would find such a feeling in the middle of a hurricane with a virtual stranger, was like a gift.

When his face was directly over hers, his mouth just a kiss away from hers, he looked into her eyes and said, "Because I see shadows in your pretty eyes, Terry." He kissed her. "Have from the first time I saw you. And I want to know what caused them." He dropped another brief, gentle kiss on her lips.

Nodding, she stared up into his deep blue eyes and fell into memory. Fell into the past that she kept too close and yet at a distance.

Running one hand idly up and down his rib cage, she spoke softly, quietly, words tumbling from her in a rush, as if they'd been banked up inside her for too long. "My family's rich. *Really* rich."

"Okay…"

"My older brother was the heir apparent. I was the princess. The debutante, the good girl who did everything right."

He kissed her again as encouragement.

"Until I was seventeen. I fell in love. With the son of my father's friend."

"You got pregnant."

"I did." And she clearly remembered the panic. The fear. The excitement and terror of knowing that she carried a child. Mistakes like unplanned pregnancies just didn't happen in the Evans family. There, everything was planned, thought out, arranged. Babies were neither expected nor wanted.

"The baby's father was scared."

"And you weren't?"

She smiled and patted his back in thanks for his solidarity. "Terrified," she assured him. "When I told my parents, they hit the eighteen-foot ceilings. They told me that I was a disappointment, but that they would take care of this 'episode' for me so no one would know."

Amazing, but her heart could still ache over that long-ago night. Scared, she'd faced her parents, knowing they'd be upset, but secretly hoping for support. Understanding.

She'd received neither.

"They arranged for an abortion. They couldn't have an unwed teenage mother in the family and they didn't want me to marry Randolph."

He snorted. "Randolph. Weenie name."

She laughed, surprising herself. "Randolph *was* a weenie. Didn't mean to be. But he'd been bred to it. And, he was young, too. Anyway…" She shook her head, jostling herself back on track. "I refused the abortion so they agreed to send me to Paris. To stay with my aunt until the baby was born. Then I would give him up for adoption."

"But you couldn't."

A single tear spilled from the corner of her eyes. "I couldn't. He was born and he came out and looked at me as if he knew me. He smiled. And he was *mine.*"

Aidan kissed her again and swiped that tear from her cheek with his thumb.

"I told my parents that I was keeping him. They told me I couldn't come home. So I stayed. In Paris with my aunt for a while, then I used my inheritance from my grandmother. Got an apartment and loved my son."

They were heady days. Filled with love and laughter and a sprinkle of fear for the future. But she wouldn't have traded a moment with Eric. Not one second. He was *love.* More love than she'd ever known before. She hadn't realized that she could feel so deeply, so profoundly.

Eric was a tiny, helpless package of love who touched her in ways she had never known existed before him. He was her world. Until…

"Terry?" His voice came, a murmur of sympathy and comfort, whispered close by her ear. "What happened?"

She closed her eyes, steeling herself against the memory, but closing her eyes only made the pictures stronger, sharper. "He was five months old. One morning, he didn't wake me up. I slept until nine and woke up thinking, *Great. He's finally sleeping through the night. Won't this make life easier?*" She bit down hard on her bottom lip, looked him in the eyes again and said, "I went in and said 'Good morning, sleepy boy' and I touched him." She was back in that sun-washed apartment. She could feel the soft breeze slipping in through the partially opened window in Eric's nursery. She heard the gentle tinkle of the wind chimes she'd hung on the terrace. She *saw* her baby. "He didn't move. Didn't stir."

"Ah, God…"

She swallowed the knot in her throat. "I remember thinking. *That's strange.* And I bent over to kiss him awake. He was cold."

"Terry…"

She brought herself up out of the past with a jerk. She couldn't stay there. Couldn't relive the rest of it. The hysterical tears, the screams for help, the sirens and the firemen and the policemen and her neighbors…all looking at her with sympathy. With tears on their faces and dread in their eyes.

"The doctor said it was SIDS. Nothing could have been done. He just…slipped away in the night."

"Jesus, Terry, I'm *so sorry.*"

"I know…"

He kissed her and tasted her tears. She felt his heat, his comfort, his need and let it swamp her, bring her from the past into a present filled with hunger and passion and *life.*

Then he went deathly still, lifted his head and looked at her through horrified eyes.

"What is it?"

"I can't believe I did this…*we* did this. Never happened to me before, I swear."

"What?"

"Talking about Eric made me think of it. Protection, Terry. We didn't use protection. Either time." His features screwed up into a mask of misery. "And now, knowing what I know, I can't believe I let you risk…"

"Hush." She laid her fingertips on his mouth, silencing him. Her own heart was pounding. She hadn't thought once about protection, either, and she of all people should have known better. But it didn't matter. As long as he was healthy, it didn't matter.

"I take the pill. To regulate my periods."

His forehead dropped to hers. "That's good." Then he rose again to look into her eyes. "I'm healthy. Don't worry about that. I'm a careful man."

"That's good to know," she said softly, catching his face between her palms. His deep blue eyes flashed with emotions she was too wrung-out to try to decipher. And right now, it wasn't important. Right now, she wanted to feel that rush of life pulsing through her again. Feel her own heartbeat race. Feel Aidan's body moving on hers.

"I'm healthy, too," she assured him, then stroked his cheekbones with her thumbs. "Now, I want you to make love with me again. And, Aidan…"

"Yeah?"

"Don't be careful of me."

Ten

The next few days passed in a blur of activity. The brunt of the hurricane skipped Baywater, moving along the coast, drenching them in high winds and torrential rain, but sparing the little town what could have been disastrous damage.

Yet, there was a lot of cleanup to do. Aidan's team was kept busy, helping the local police and fire department on several calls. He called to check on his family's safety, but didn't have time to actually get together with his brothers. Until tonight. Between his regular duties on the base and the SAR runs his team was making, he was kept pretty much at a run.

And whatever down time he *did* have, he spent with Terry.

He couldn't seem to get enough of her. Since that first night of the storm, they'd been together every night. Making love, talking, laughing, arguing. He'd never spent so much time with a woman before without feeling the need to bolt.

Always, before Terry, Aidan had kept his distance— at least emotionally. He'd never wanted to *know* a woman beyond the superficial level that allowed them both to enjoy each other. Now though, there was more.

It had sneaked up on him and he wasn't entirely sure what to do about it. Drawn to her time and again, he felt himself being pulled deeper into her life, her world. A corner of his brain continually warned him to back off. To remember that his life was here, hers was in New York. That a former debutante had *nothing* in common with a career Marine.

And mostly, to remember that he wasn't *looking* for forever. That he didn't *want* love.

But that small voice in his mind was getting fainter—harder to hear.

He walked into the Lighthouse restaurant and paused just inside the entrance. He hooked his sunglasses on the open vee neck of his dark blue pullover shirt and let his gaze sweep the crowded restaurant. Families dotted the round, wooden tables, celebrating being together. Celebrating surviving the hurricane.

He spotted his brothers at a back table and braced

himself for the ragging he knew was coming his way. He'd been riding Connor and Brian hard for the last few weeks, so he fully expected to take his share of crap.

Stalking across the crowded room, he stepped up to the table and told Brian, "Move over."

When he did, Aidan dropped onto the bench seat. Shifting his gaze from Brian beside him to Connor and Liam across from him, he took a breath and said, "I'm out."

Whoops and delighted laughter rolled out from the other three men and got loud enough that people at the other tables turned to stare.

Aidan hunched his shoulders. "Jeez. Keep it down, will ya?"

"This is great," Connor said, still laughing.

Brian held up one hand and leaned across the table. Connor slapped that hand hard and they whooped again, just for the hell of it. Liam grinned and rubbed his own palms together as if he were already getting ready to count the money he and the church had just won.

"So what happened?" Brian demanded, giving Aidan a hard elbow to the ribs.

"What? You need a picture? You know damn well what happened."

"Yeah, but what happened to all your big talk about outlasting us?"

"I *did* outlast you two losers," Aidan reminded him quickly. He might not have won the bet, but he'd sure as hell beat out the other two members of the Reilly triplets.

"Yeah, man," Connor said, folding his arms on the table top. "But you only had two weeks to go. I really thought you were gonna pull it off."

"Not me," Brian muttered.

"Terry?" Liam asked quietly.

Aidan just nodded.

"Terry?" Connor repeated, straightening up and looking around the table like a man who's the only one not in on a joke. "Who the hell's Terry?"

"Yeah," Brian added, glaring at Liam. "How is it *you* know about this chick and we don't?"

"You guys don't know everything," Aidan muttered, sliding down in his seat.

"Here you go, guys," a woman's voice said cheerfully, "four draft beers."

The Reilly brothers shut up fast while the waitress delivered their drinks and didn't start talking again until after she was gone.

Aidan reached for his beer and took a long, deep swig. The icy froth hit the back of his throat and eased down the knot of irritation lodged there.

"So spill," Connor demanded. "Who's the new babe?"

"She's not a 'babe,'" Aidan told him, wincing slightly, since he called Terry "babe" all the damn time.

"Where'd you meet her? The Off Duty?" Brian laughed.

He had a right to laugh, Aidan supposed. Usually the women he met *did* hang out at the bar that catered to Marines.

He took another drink, then explained how he'd met Terry. And in telling his brothers, he relived it all. He didn't notice, but his voice softened, his eyes shone and his features lit with warmth.

"She sounds…special," Liam said when Aidan stopped talking.

Snapping his gaze to his older brother, Aidan fought down a sudden, near-overpowering flash of panic. Glancing from Liam to Brian and finally to Connor, he shook his head. "Don't start with me, you guys. Don't make more of this than there is."

"I didn't say anything," Connor pointed out, lifting both hands in mock surrender.

"You didn't have to. I can see it on your face."

"You ought to be looking at *your* face," Brian pointed out and took a drink of his own beer.

"What's that supposed to mean?" Aidan argued.

"Hell, man," Brian said, "holster it. Loving a woman's nothing to be ashamed of." He grinned. "Well, except for Liam."

"Funny," their older brother said and leaned across the table to slap Brian upside the head.

"Hey!"

"Stand down," Aidan told all of them, his voice low pitched but steady and firm. "Nobody said anything about *love* for God's sake. All I'm admitting to is losing the stupid bet."

"Relax, man," Connor said, picking up his beer and gesturing with it. "We've all been there—except for Liam."

"I have to take this from you, too?" Liam growled.

Connor shrugged.

"Seriously," Aidan said, feeling the snaky, cold tentacles of panic tighten just a bit around his insides, "shut the hell up about love. I'm not in love. Don't plan to be in love. You guys can have it."

"You make it sound like a disease or something," Brian said.

"Isn't it?" Aidan countered.

"What crawled up your ass and died?" Connor grumbled.

"Yeah," Liam asked, his voice quieter, more thoughtful. "What's got you so scared, Aidan?"

Instantly he bristled. "Didn't say I was scared, for God's sake. Just said I wasn't interested."

"Don't know why the hell not," Brian said. "Hell, can't imagine not being married to Tina."

"Oh, yeah," Aidan sniped. "You liked marriage to Tina so much, you divorced her *then* remarried her."

"You want to go a round with me?" his brother snarled.

"He's just itchy," Connor cut in, breaking up the tension before it could spiral into one of the Reilly brothers' world famous knock-down-drag-out fights.

"Hell, I remember how it felt. I love Emma, but damned if I wanted to admit it—even to myself."

"Now you're both married," Aidan grumbled. "And what'd it get you?"

"Happiness?" Liam offered.

"No offense, Liam," Aidan said, snapping him a look. "But priests don't get a vote in this."

An angry flush swept up his older brother's face, then faded again almost instantly. "I may be a priest, Aidan, but I'm also a man. *And* your brother."

"*And,* you know jack about women." Aidan took another long drink, set his beer down onto the table and cupped the frosty glass between his palms. Staring at the pale gold liquid, he muttered, "These two at least have a position to argue from. You don't. You don't know what it is to—" he caught himself before uttering the 'L' word "—*care* about someone. To know she matters and also know that you can't let her matter too much."

"Got you there, Liam," Brian pointed out.

"Too true," Connor added. "You lucked out. Didn't have to worry about pissing a woman off and living with the results."

"Who the hell do you three think you're talking to?" Liam demanded, but focused on Aidan, leaning across the table, forcing Connor back in his seat, a surprised expression on his face. "Do you think I was *born* wearing this collar?" he tapped at the white circlet at his throat. "I was your brother first. I was a man first. Do you really believe I never loved any-one? That I don't know what it feels like to *want?*"

Aidan just blinked at him. It had been years since he'd seen that flash fire of fury in Liam's eyes.

"Take it easy, Liam," Brian urged, shooting a glance at the table closest to them and glaring the nosy woman sitting there a narrowed glance.

"You shut up," Liam growled. "This is between me and the moron."

"Hey."

"My turn, idiot. You shut up and listen." Liam pointed one finger at Aidan, took a breath and low-ered his voice. "I was in love once."

"What?" All three triplets said it at once.

Liam's eyes didn't flicker. His gaze didn't shift. Just held Aidan's steadily.

"Her name was Ailish."

"Whoa," Connor murmured.

"I thought priests *heard* confessions…" Brian said softly.

"I met her in Ireland," Liam continued as if none of them had spoken. "That last summer before I went into the seminary."

Aidan thought back, remembering the trip Liam had taken while trying to decide if he was really cut out for a life in the priesthood. He'd stayed in their grandparents' house outside Galway and toured Ire-land for a summer. He'd never really talked about those three months, and the rest of them had let it go, assuming that Liam had spent those months in quiet reflection and prayer.

Apparently, they were wrong.

Aidan kept his gaze locked with Liam's, unable to look away. "What happened, Liam? If you loved her so damn much, why'd you let her go?"

Liam's breath hissed in and out of him in rapid succession. His eyes glimmered brightly, then darkened in memory. Slowly, he eased back into his seat, still staring at Aidan. "She died."

"Ah, Liam." Connor murmured.

"Damn, Liam…" Brian winced in sympathy.

Aidan held his breath. Sure there was more. He watched his older brother relive old pain and wondered how they'd drifted into this minefield of emotion.

"She drove into Galway city to meet her sister for some shopping," Liam said softly. "An American tourist got confused, drove on the wrong side of the road. Hit her head-on. She was killed instantly."

God.

"I'm sorry, Liam," Aidan said, stunned to his soul. In all these years, his brother had never hinted at the tragedy that must haunt him still. And Aidan finally realized that Marines weren't the only people with courage.

Anger gone now, Liam smiled sadly. "It was a long time ago, Aidan. And I'm only telling you guys now because I want you to know I *do* understand. I know what it is to love a woman so much that she's all you can see of tomorrow."

Silence dropped on the four of them like an old quilt. Each of them lost in their own thoughts, none of them wanted to be the first to speak.

Naturally enough, it was Connor who finally shattered the quiet.

"So, if Ailish had lived," he asked, slanting a glance at Liam, "would you still have become a priest? Or would you have walked away from her?"

Liam's hand fisted around his glass of beer. He lifted it, took a long sip and set it back down again before answering. "I've asked myself that a thousand times over the years," he admitted, then looked from one brother to the other, each in turn. "The honest answer is, no. I wouldn't have. When I met her, it was as if God had sent me a sign, telling me that He didn't want me in the priesthood after all." He sighed again, wistfully. "We planned to be married in the local church. Get a house near Lough Mask. Then when she was gone…"

"Married?" Aidan's voice was a whisper, carrying the stunned surprise all of them felt.

It took another moment or two before Liam smiled again. "I still believe there's a reason for everything—though I've yet to find the reason for her death. But maybe meeting Ailish, *loving* Ailish was supposed to help me be a better priest."

"I don't know what to say," Brian looked at their oldest brother.

"You don't have to say anything," Liam told them all.

An uneasy silence dropped over them. All of them aware now of Liam's private little hell—none of them quite sure how to handle this new side to a brother they thought they'd known.

Finally Brian spoke up again and, thank God, changed the subject. "You are a good priest, you know."

Liam glanced at him. "Thanks. I think."

"No, I mean it," Brian said and took a drink of his own beer. "Which means, I can probably use a few of those super prayers you've got in your stash."

"What's going on?" Connor asked the question they were all thinking.

"I'm shipping out." Brian looked at each of them in turn, then shrugged and grinned. "Next month. Middle East."

Growing up with a Marine father had taught them all that sudden moves were to be expected. Growing up a *family* made them all feel that instant quiver of worry.

"Have you told Tina yet?" Liam asked.

"Nope," Brian admitted. "I'm going home to do that now. That's why I thought I'd ask for those prayers." He grinned again. "Combat's dangerous, but fighting with Tina can be deadly."

"But you'll still be here for our joint humiliation, right?" Connor asked.

"Oh, yeah. Battle Color day. Convertible. Hula

skirt, coconut bra. I'll be there." He gave Aidan a shove. "Slide out, will you?"

"I'll walk out with you," Connor said, "Gotta be getting home or Emma'll hunt me down like a dog."

Aidan snorted a laugh. "See? This is what married gets you. A woman ready to tear your lungs out."

Brian shook his head. "You really *are* an idiot, aren't you?" Then he punched one fist into Aidan's shoulder. "Move."

Aidan got to his feet and Brian slid across the bench seat and stood up beside him. Pulling a couple of bills from his pocket, he tossed them onto the table and said, "See you guys later."

Then he and Connor headed out and Aidan sat back down. "Tina's not going to be happy about this."

Liam shrugged. "She's strong. She'll worry about him, but she'll handle it."

"I suppose." But Aidan wasn't really thinking about his sister-in-law, or even about Brian, soon to be deploying into a combat situation.

Instead he was thinking about his older brother and the love he'd lost so long ago. Looking at Liam, he asked, "Why'd you tell us about her?"

Liam sighed and leaned back in his seat. "I don't know. Maybe I was just tired of hearing about how I don't know jack about women."

Aidan smiled briefly and nodded. "Okay. I can get that."

This news was still too fresh to make much sense

of. He'd always thought of Liam as a quiet, reflective man. Born for the priesthood. Now, to discover there'd been dreams born and lost along the way was a little…disquieting.

"What was she like?"

"Ailish?"

"Yes."

Liam smiled sadly. "Beautiful. Warm. Funny. Stubborn." His voice softened in memory. "She was an artist, too. Damn good one. Landscapes mostly."

A lightbulb clicked on in Aidan's brain. "The painting in your room. The one of the standing stones."

"Yeah. That's one of hers."

Aidan had always liked that painting. Had even tried to buy it from Liam once. Now he knew why his brother had refused to part with it. A simple scene of a circle of standing stones, a dance, as the Irish called them, it had a mystical quality, with soft gray mist spilling across the emerald green grass and twining itself up around the stones like loving hands.

"She was good."

Liam smiled. "I don't need you to feel sorry for me, Aidan."

"What am I supposed to feel, then?"

Liam leaned across the table and smiled patiently. "I just want you to *think*." He pulled money from his pocket, tossed it onto the table and said, "Think about

what you've found. What you *could* have. And think
hard before you let yourself lose it."

Then he left.

And Aidan sat alone, not sure of anything anymore.

Eleven

"**I** can come home early."

"You don't have to do that," Terry said, clutching the phone receiver as she walked around the kitchen, pouring herself some iced tea. "Honestly, Donna, everything's fine."

"No damage to the store? The house?"

Terry sighed. She'd already reassured her friend a half dozen times over the last few days. But she supposed it wasn't easy to be thousands of miles away from home when disaster struck.

"There was a small leak in the bookstore," she told her again. "A *tiny* puddle in the back, by the kids' play area."

"Damn it. Should have had the roof fixed last year. I *knew* that and put it off anyway."

"It's a *very* tiny leak, Donna. Honestly. The store did not float away."

"Okay, okay, I know I'm being a little obsessive…"

"Just a tad," Terry agreed, smiling as she closed the refrigerator door and picked up the glass of tea off the table. Taking a sip, she said, "Just enjoy the rest of your time with your folks."

"To tell you the truth, they're jumping up and down on my last nerve."

Terry laughed, pulled out a chair and sat down. God it felt good to think about something else besides her own situation. Her brain had been running in circles over Aidan Reilly for days—and she *still* had no idea how to handle what was getting to be a more and more complicated relationship.

Of course, to Aidan, it probably wasn't complicated at all, she thought wryly. It was her own fault she'd made the mistake of feeling more than she should have. Now she just had to figure out what to do about it.

"Don't get me wrong," Donna said, "my parents are great. But they spend all their time giving the kids chocolate, which hypes the little tormentors into outer space and then they drive me insane."

A sigh of regret whispered through Terry as she wondered what her life would be now, if Eric had only lived. He'd be twelve now. Almost a teenager. She closed her eyes and tried to imagine that sweet baby face as it would be now, and couldn't quite pull it off.

She'd always wanted children. At one time, she'd assumed she'd have a houseful of them. Now, it looked as though those dreams had been buried with Eric. She was alone. And despite what she felt for Aidan, she was going to stay alone.

Shaking her head a little, she said, "Sounds like things're just the way they're supposed to be then."

"I guess. I'm just ready to be home."

"Yeah," Terry said softly. "So am I."

"Tired of small-town life?" Donna asked. "Ready to go back to Manhattan and start whipping those fund-raisers into shape again?"

Truthfully, Terry thought, but didn't say, *no*. She liked Baywater. She liked having neighbors, even though they were only on loan from Donna. She liked the small-town feel, the slower pace, the sense of community she'd experienced when the hurricane swept through.

And mostly, she liked Aidan.

Instantly that quick grin of his filled her mind. His dimple. The deep, stormy blue of his eyes. The gravelly voice in the middle of the night. The callused fingertips sliding over her skin. His laugh. His humor and strength.

She liked it all.

Oh dear God.

She'd really done it.

She'd fallen in love.

Sitting up straight in the ladder-back chair, she stared blankly at the wall opposite her. Why hadn't she noticed this when there was still time to prevent it?

But then, maybe she'd never had a chance against it. She'd felt something new, something incredibly strong and powerful from the first moment they'd met.

She'd known then that he was different. That he could be dangerous.

She just hadn't realized *how* dangerous.

"Hello? Earth to Terry, come in, Terry."

"Huh? Oh." Shaking her head, she grabbed up her tea, took a long drink and swallowed the icy liquid and felt the chill of it swamp her right down to the bone.

But it wasn't the tea giving her the shivers.

It was the knowledge that she'd given her heart to a man who wouldn't want it.

"Oh, no."

"What? What's wrong?" Donna demanded.

"Oh, I've made a big mistake."

"Sounds bad."

"Couldn't be worse."

"And is the name of this mistake Aidan?"

"How'd you guess?"

"Not really a big jump," Donna admitted, and she couldn't hide the delight in her voice.

"You don't have to sound so pleased about this," Terry muttered, grimacing at the phone she was clutching tightly enough to snap in two.

"Why wouldn't I be pleased? Two of my closest friends find true love and happiness? This is good news."

"Hah!" Terry leaned back in her chair. "As far as Aidan's concerned, we've found sweaty sex and completion."

"And you?"

She sighed. "Donna…I'm an idiot."

"No, you're not, sweetie," her friend crooned. "You fell in love. That makes you lucky."

"No. It just makes it harder to leave."

"You're not going to *stay* and see what happens?"

"Nope." Terry stood up, walked to the window and stared out at the sun splashed backyard. The sky was blue, white clouds drifted lazily across the sky and a puff of wind teased the brass chimes into a soft tune. It was as if the hurricane had never come.

And she knew, that once she was home, buried in work, in the familiar, this feeling for Aidan would go away, too, and it would be like these few weeks had never been.

If a part of her was saddened at the thought, it was just a small part. The hard reality was, she didn't want to love someone again. Didn't want to risk loss again.

After Eric's death, Terry had been lost. Devastated. She'd spiraled into an overwhelming need for risk. She'd put her life on the line time and again, chasing down thrills, adventure.

She hadn't really taken the time then to realize that

she had been, in a way, chasing death. Her own life had felt inconsolably lonely. She'd missed her son desperately and hadn't reconciled with her family enough to find comfort there.

Instead she'd jumped into a whirlwind of activity that was dangerous enough that it kept her mind too busy to grieve. Her heart too full to break.

Until that one morning five years ago. Waking up in that hospital bed, she'd finally faced the sad truth. That she'd become as empty as her world had felt. That she'd chased danger so she wouldn't have to face life without her baby. And that was a slap in the face to the love she'd found with Eric.

Since that morning, she'd changed. Built a life that was based on giving. On helping. On reaching out a hand to those who felt as alone as she once had.

But if she were to chance loving Aidan, wouldn't she be going back into the danger zone? Wouldn't she be handing the universe another opportunity to kick her in the teeth?

"Terry?"

"Sorry," she murmured, still half lost in thought.

"You're really shook, aren't you?"

"Yeah, I guess I am," she admitted, grateful at least to have this one old friend to talk to. To confess her fears and worries to.

"You know what? I'm coming home early."

"You don't have to do that," Terry said.

"I know. But I miss my own place anyway."

"Donna…"

"I'll be there tomorrow or the next day."

"Okay," she said, already planning her return to Manhattan. She wasn't running, she told herself firmly. She was retreating. Quickly. "And, Donna?"

"Yeah?"

"Thanks."

Two hours later, Liam opened the door to the rectory himself.

The housekeeper was out doing the weekly grocery shopping and the monsignor was in the church hearing confessions. Which left Liam to wait for the roofer to arrive and give them an estimate.

But when he opened the door, he didn't find Mr. Angelini. Instead a tall, curvy blonde with summer-green eyes and a quiet smile greeted him. Instantly he knew who she must be.

"You're Terry Evans."

"Father Liam Reilly?" she asked with a smile. "Aidan didn't tell me his brother was psychic."

"Oh, I'm not," Liam said, opening the door wider and waving one hand in invitation. "But Aidan's described you too well to be mistaken on this."

She stepped into the foyer, her cream colored heels making quiet clicks on the gleaming wooden floor. Liam closed the door, then faced her, a beautiful woman in an expensive, beige suit and yellow silk blouse. She looked…uneasy and Liam's instincts took over.

"Can I get you something cold to drink? We have soda, which I would recommend over my housekeeper's hideous iced tea."

"No. Nothing, thanks," she said and walked with him into the living room off the hall.

"Please. Sit down."

She took a seat on the sofa and Liam perched on the coffee table in front of her. There was unhappiness in her eyes and a wistful quality about her that tugged on his heart. Now he understood why Aidan had fallen so fast and so hard. The wonder of it to him was that the man was still struggling so against it.

"What brings you here, Terry?"

She inhaled sharply and looked around the room before shifting her gaze back to his. "Direct. I like that."

He nodded, waiting.

"Aidan told me," she said, "that you were going to use the ten thousand dollars from the bet to replace the church's roof."

He smiled. "Did he?"

She opened her purse, dug inside for an envelope, then pulled it out and studied it. "I don't know if you know this already, but he had planned to give you the money anyway, even if he had won that stupid bet."

His eyebrows lifted. "No, I didn't know. But it sounds like something Aidan would do. He's a good man."

"Yes," she said, running her fingertips idly across the back of the envelope. "He is."

"And you love him."

Her gaze snapped up to his and Liam smiled. Even if he hadn't been expecting it, he would have spotted the sharp jolt of emotion in her eyes. And it made him glad for Aidan. It was high time his brother found something that meant as much to him as the Corps did.

"You sure you're not psychic?" she asked, giving him a wary smile.

"Oh, I'm sure. But if you don't mind my saying so, it's easy enough to read your eyes."

"Great. I'm an open book." Terry shrugged slightly. "I hope Aidan's not in a *reading* mood."

"You don't want him to know?"

"No," she said it softly, firmly. "Neither one of us was looking for this, Father—"

"Liam," he corrected.

"—Liam. What happened between us...well. It doesn't matter."

"You're a lot like him," Liam said.

She laughed shortly. "No reason to be insulting."

He grinned, liking this woman more and more and wanting to kick Aidan's ass for even taking the chance of losing her.

"Anyway," she said, "that's not why I'm here."

"Okay, then why?" he asked, bracing his forearms on his thighs and leaning in toward her.

"For this," she said and handed him the envelope.

Confused now, Liam opened it, looked inside and stared in stunned shock. Her personal check for twenty-five thousand dollars, made out to St. Sebastian's, was nestled inside.

Lifting his gaze to hers, he said, "Not that we don't appreciate the donation, we do. But that's a big check. Can I ask what motivated it?"

She snapped her small purse closed again and folded her hands on top of it. "Ten thousand wouldn't have been enough to get you a new roof, Liam."

"True, but that doesn't explain your generosity."

She inhaled sharply. "Let's just say that I've come to like Baywater." She jumped to her feet and walked briskly across the room to stare out the front windows at the trees that lined the driveway. "It's a nice place. Nice people. I'm going to miss it. And I wanted to help in some way, before I left town."

"You're leaving?"

She turned to look at him nodded, and looked down, but not before Liam saw the gleam of regret in her eyes.

"When?"

"A day or two."

"Does Aidan know?"

"No—and I'd like your promise that you won't tell him."

"Are you going to?"

"I don't know yet."

Sighing, Liam set the envelope down on the table beside him, walked toward her and took both of her hands in his. "Is there some way I can help you?"

She smiled briefly and shook her head. "No, but thanks for offering."

"Are you sure you want to leave?" Liam asked, wondering how in heaven two such stubborn souls had managed to find each other.

She drew away from him and shook her head. "I didn't say I *want* to leave. Just that I am."

He smiled sadly. "That makes no sense at all, you know."

A short, harsh laugh shot from her throat. "Maybe not. But its something I have to do."

"Maybe you should tell Aidan how you feel."

Now she did laugh. "Oh, no." Shaking her head she said, "Even if I was willing to take a chance on love again—you know as well as I do that Aidan's not interested."

"He cares for you."

"Yes. I think he really does." She started past him, headed for the front door. "But it's not love, Father. He doesn't want that any more than I do."

"Are you sure about that?"

"Sure enough."

Liam followed her to the front door. She opened it before he could and then stepped out onto the small porch, shaded by a climbing wisteria vine.

"Thank you again," he said, "for your donation."

"You're welcome, Liam. It was nice meeting you," she said and took the two steps to the sidewalk, leading around to the parking lot behind the church.

"Terry?"

She stopped and looked back at him, bright green eyes shadowed with pain.

His jaw tightened and though his every instinct was to help, comfort, he held himself back—knowing somehow, that she wouldn't welcome it. "My brother's an idiot if he lets you get away."

She shook her head. "Sometimes, Father, getting away is kindest all around."

She left then and Liam stood in a splash of sunlight wondering how in the hell he could wake his brother up to reality before it was too late.

Twelve

Aidan smiled as he pulled into the driveway at Donna Fletcher's house. Dusk was just settling over Baywater and the sky was still streaked with dark reds and orange. A slight wind pushed at the trees and from down the street, came the shrieks of children playing. Next door, Mr. Franklin was mowing the lawn and the older man nodded and waved as Aidan stepped out of his car.

He grabbed the still hot pizza box from the passenger seat, then snatched up a bottle of merlot he'd brought to go with it. Grinning, he headed for the house.

He'd been thinking about this moment all day. Through the work, through the joking around with the other guys, in the back of his mind, Aidan had been planning a nice, quiet night, with Terry cuddled up close beside him.

Funny. A couple of weeks ago, he never would have imagined that a cozy night at home would sound so damn good. But then, a couple of weeks ago, he hadn't yet met Terry Evans.

And ever since he had, his world had taken a subtle shift.

He shook his head and sprinted the last few steps to the front porch. Didn't want to think about what he was feeling. Didn't want to examine anything too closely. Better to just shut up and enjoy it.

He used the bottom end of the wine bottle to tap on the door and when it swung open, his smile dropped like a stone.

Terry stood there, wearing a pale beige suit and high heels. Her makeup was perfect, her hair styled and surprise flickered in her green eyes. "Aidan? You said you couldn't make it tonight."

Frowning, he said, "I got Monk to cover for me."

"Oh. Well."

His brain tried to work. He could almost hear the gears grinding slowly inside his head. She wasn't expecting him, but she was dressed to the teeth and ready for…*what,* exactly?

He glanced past her then and noticed the suitcases stacked in the foyer. Ice settled in the pit of his stomach as he lifted his gaze up to hers again. "Going somewhere?"

Clearly nervous, she licked her lips, pulled in a long breath and said, "Yes. Actually, when you knocked, I thought it was my cab."

"Your *cab*."

"To take me to the airport."

"You're leaving."

"Yes. I'm going home."

"Tonight."

"Yes."

The ice in his stomach melted with a sizzle under a sudden onslaught of fury. She was looking at him as if he were a stranger. She was *leaving*. And didn't look sorry about it.

"Without even telling me?" he asked. "Without saying a damn word?"

She blew out a breath that ruffled the wisp of bangs drifting across her forehead. "Aidan, don't make this harder than it has to be."

He laughed shortly, harshly and felt it scrape his throat. "Not really sure if I could do that."

He felt like an idiot. Standing there in jeans and a T-shirt, clutching a swiftly going cold pizza and a bottle of wine—while she stood there and told him she was leaving.

Shouldn't he have known this?

Shouldn't he have *felt* something? A warning of some kind?

"So what was the plan?" he snarled. "Were you going to call from the airport? Or just let me show up here to find you gone?"

She stiffened and her lips flattened into a grim line. "Donna will be here tomorrow. She could have—"

Another laugh, tighter, harsher than the first. "That's great. You were gonna let *Donna* tell me that you were too chicken to face me."

"That's about enough."

"See? I don't think so."

He dropped the pizza and thought seriously about smashing the stupid bottle of wine against the side of the house. But instead, he tightened his fingers on the neck of the bottle and clung to it like a safety rope. "I thought we had something."

"Really?" she asked, temper clearly spiking inside her now, too. She folded her arms over her chest, hitched one hip higher than the other as she tapped the toe of her shoe against the floor. "And what did you think we had?"

That left him speechless. Hell, how did he know the answer to that? He shoved one hand across the top of his head. "I'm not sure exactly. But whatever the hell it is, it was worth more than *this*."

Disappointment flashed in her eyes briefly and was gone again in an instant. In fact, he couldn't really be sure he'd seen it at all.

"Aidan, go home. This little…interlude is over. Let's just get back to our lives, okay?"

"Just like that?"

Behind him, he heard a car pull up and the short blast of a horn.

"That's my cab."

He turned around to glare at it, and when he looked back, Terry already had her suitcase on the porch and was closing and locking the door. He felt as though he was back in the hurricane. As though the world was suddenly moving too quickly for him to keep up.

He knew he should say something, *do* something, but instead he stood there like a moron as she walked past him, rolling her suitcase behind her, its small steel wheels grinding against the pavement.

He was still standing there when the driver opened the passenger door to usher her into the bright yellow cab. She stopped, hand on the door's edge, to look at him. Then she gave him a ghost of a smile and said, "Goodbye, Aidan."

Alone with his wine and his stone cold pizza, Aidan watched in silence as Terry drove out of his life.

Two weeks later, the Reilly brothers were considering voting Aidan out of the family.

"My point," he yelled as he grabbed the rebounded basketball and took off at a trot toward the end of the driveway.

"Your point because you fouled me," Brian snapped.

"It wasn't a foul."

"It was a *shove*," Connor told him.

Aidan sighed, wiped his arm across his forehead and sneered at his brothers. "Sorry, girls. Didn't know I was being too rough."

"You know," Brian said, starting for him, "I'm thinking it's about time for somebody's clock to get cleaned."

Aidan tossed the ball to one side, braced himself and waved one hand. "Bring it on, tough guy."

"What the hell's wrong with you, Aidan?" Connor demanded, grabbing Brian's arm as he started past him.

"*Nothing's* wrong with me. You two are the ones doing all the griping."

Liam picked up the basketball, bounced it a couple of times and nodded at Connor and Brian. "You two go get a beer. I need to talk to Aidan."

The other two stalked off, muttering darkly and Aidan turned, walking toward the water bottle he'd tossed down an hour ago. Grabbing it, he uncapped it, took a long gulp then fired a warning look at Liam. "I don't want to hear it."

"Tough."

Aidan snorted.

"You miss her."

Aidan stilled. His hand fisted on the water bottle and he stared at it as if it held the secrets of the universe.

"Shut up, Liam."

"Not a chance. You're making a jackass of yourself and driving your brothers to plan your murder. When are you going to admit you love her?"

He shot his oldest brother a hot glare. "This is none of your business, Liam. So back the hell off."

The sun was hot and the air didn't stir. It felt heavy, thick. And too damned crowded around there for Aidan's comfort.

"You're my business, you idiot." Liam moved in close, shoved Aidan and demanded, "Do you think we don't know what's going on? Do you think nobody's noticed that ever since Terry left you've been a complete beast to be around?"

Fury spiked inside him, then just as quickly drained away. Hell. Liam was right. They were *all* right. With Terry gone, nothing felt good. There was no reason to get up in the morning and going to sleep brought no comfort because his dreams were filled with her. Then he'd awaken in the dark with empty arms and a hollow heart.

"She's the one who left," he pointed out in a dark murmur.

"Did you give her a reason to stay?"

"No." He'd wanted to. Wanted to say something that day on the porch. Wanted to tell her…*hell.*

Still clutching the water bottle, he dropped to the shaded grass, drew his knees up and rested his forearms atop them. When Liam took a seat nearby, Aidan started talking. "Just before Uncle Patrick died," he said, peeling the label from the bottle of water, "and left us the money that started this whole mess…"

"Yeah?"

"I went to see him. About a week before he died. Just before I left, he took my hand and he said—" Aidan closed his eyes, to recapture that moment clearly "—the worst part of dying, Aidan, is to die with regrets. Don't make the mistake I did. Do all you can. See all you can. Don't die being sorry for what you *didn't* do."

"I'm sorry he felt that way. He lived a good life," Liam said.

"Yeah, but he lived a quiet life. He never went anywhere, never did anything. I don't want to be that way." He shook his head firmly. "Don't want to die with regrets, Liam."

"And this has what to do with Terry?" His brother asked.

"Don't you get it? If I let myself be in love, I'm tying myself down. Giving up the space to explore, to dare, to risk."

Liam stared at him for a long minute, then shook his head and laughed. "Every time I think maybe you're not a moron, you prove me wrong."

"Thanks," Aidan muttered. "That's helpful."

"Did it ever occur to you that Uncle Patrick might have meant something else?"

"Huh?"

"He never married, remember? Lived by himself most of his life, kept to himself. Mom says he was a shy man in his younger days, so maybe that explains some of it."

"Your point?"

"My point is, Aidan, maybe the regrets he spoke of were more about what he'd missed emotionally in his life. Maybe he regretted never being in love. Never finding a woman to cherish. Never having children."

He hadn't really considered that before.

"Yeah," Aidan said, "but…"

"Aidan," Liam continued, stretching his long legs out in front of him, "you've already done more in your life than most people ever will."

"True."

"Do you really believe, being the kind of man you are, that having someone to love and to love you, would change all that?"

"Well…" His brain was working now, circling around, backing up, going forward again. Trying to shift all of Liam's words into an order that didn't come off making him feel so damn stupid.

It wasn't working.

"Love doesn't *end* your life, Aidan," Liam said, snatching his brother's water bottle away and taking a drink. "It makes it *better*. If you're smart enough to grab it when you have the chance."

"Yeah," Aidan said, feeling the first trickle of hope seep into him like a slow stream in high summer. "But what if she doesn't want me? What if she tells me to get lost?"

Liam snorted now. "Since when do you turn your back on a challenge?" He smiled. "Besides, I don't think she'll turn you away. Before she left, she gave me a check for twenty-five thousand dollars. For the church's roof."

"She did?" Stunned, Aidan stared at him. "Why?"

"She said it was because she liked Baywater and wanted to help. I think it's because she loves *you* and wanted to feel somehow a part of things here, even if she was leaving."

Aidan thought about it for several humming seconds, then jumped to his feet. Glaring at Aidan, he shouted, "Well why the hell didn't you say so?"

Liam laughed as Aidan ran all the way to his car, jumped inside and roared off.

Terry set her teacup down on the polished mahogany table and the click of fine china on wood sounded like thunder in the quiet penthouse. If she listened hard enough, she could probably hear the pounding of her own heart. It was too damn quiet. Too lonely. Too…*empty.*

But at least it wouldn't be that way for long.

The last two weeks had been a small eternity. Back on her home turf, she'd tried to step right back into her normal everyday rhythm. But it was no use. It wasn't the same, because *she* wasn't the same.

She'd changed. And there was no going back— even if she'd wanted to.

When the doorbell rang, she ran for it. Her socks hit the polished marble floor and she slid all the way to the wide double doors. Laughing at herself, she opened the door and froze.

Aidan stepped inside, closed the door and grabbed her.

Held up close to his chest, she felt his heartbeat thundering against her and she knew she'd never felt anything more wonderful in her life. Being in his arms again set her world right. Everything felt in balance again. As it should be.

As it was meant to be.

"Aidan," She managed to say, "What're you—"

"Just shut up a minute, okay?" He blurted it out, then held her back so he could look at her, staring into her eyes with an intensity that burned right down to the heart of her. "God, you look good."

She smiled and would have spoken, but he rushed right on, not giving her a chance.

"I came all the way here to tell you something." He took a deep breath, blew it out and blurted, "I *love* you, Terry. And I want you to love me back."

"Aidan—"

"Look," he plowed on, outshouting her, "I know why you've protected your heart so long. I understand. About Eric. About all of it."

Her eyes filled with tears, but she blinked them back, unwilling to have this vision of him blurred.

"But you can't do it forever, Terry. I finally understand that. Look, I risk my life everyday in my job. And I never minded before, because I really didn't have all that much to lose. Well now, I *do*. I'll keep taking the risks, because that's the job and it's a risk worth taking. But so is loving you."

Her heart swelled to bursting and her chest felt too tight to contain it. "Oh, Aidan, I—"

"Terry, I'm not the same guy I was when I met you." His blue eyes went dark and stormy, filled with emotion that reached out for her and shook her to the soles of her feet. "You've affected my work, my life. You filled my heart. I don't want to wake up another morning without you. I need you, Terry. And I hope you need me."

"Oh, Aidan…"

"I know love and marriage and all the rest of it is a *big* risk. But I want us to take it together. Can you do it, Terry? Can you love me? Marry me?"

His fingers tightened on her upper arms and she was grateful for his firm grip. Otherwise, she might have melted into a puddle at his feet.

Smiling up at him, she said, "Yes, I love you. And yes, I'll marry you. Today. Tomorrow. Whenever you want. Because I'm not the same, either. You filled me, when I thought I would never be whole again. And the last two weeks without you were emptier than anything I've ever known."

"Thank God," he muttered and pulled her close again. Wrapping his arms around her, he bent his head to the curve of her neck and inhaled the soft, floral fragrance of her. And for the first time since the evening she'd left, Aidan felt his heart beating again.

"There's something else you should know though," she whispered and he pulled back to look at her, waiting.

"I'm pregnant."

Stunned, he blinked at her. "But. You said. The pill. We. You."

She grinned and shrugged. "Apparently, they're not a hundred percent effective."

"Yeah. But. I."

"I was coming to see you, Aidan, to tell you. When you rang the bell, I thought it was the realtor come to list the penthouse."

"You were coming back to me?" he asked with a smile.

"Yeah," she said softly. "I was going to find a way to *make* you love me."

"Babe," he said, inhaling sharply and grinning now to flash that dimple at her. "You already did that."

He pulled her in close again and whispered into her hair. "I'm happy about the baby, Terry. Terrified, but really happy. But are you okay with it? I mean, after Eric. Aren't you scared?"

She nestled in close and felt her fears dissolve in a well of love. She had been scared. When the pregnancy test turned up positive, fear reared up and nibbled on her. But then she realized that if loving Eric prevented her from ever loving another child, then she was cheating both herself and the memory of her son.

"Yeah," she admitted quietly. "I'm a little scared. But I'm also *alive,* Aidan. For the first time in a long time, I'm really *alive.*"

She pulled her head back and looked up at him. "I want to love you, Aidan. Laugh with you. Fight with you. Build a family with you."

He brought his hands up to cup her face and smiled down at her. "You'll never be sorry you took a chance on me, Terry. I swear it."

"We took a chance on each other," she whispered and leaned in to meet his kiss.

Epilogue

Two days later, the sun was sinking against the horizon. Most of the speeches were finished, the Marine band was tuning up and the grounds were packed. There were never enough bleacher seats, so most people just brought lawn chairs and blankets, spreading out across the area.

Battle Color Day, when every Marine dignitary available was on hand for the Corps celebration.

The speeches were mercifully brief, the Drum and Bugle Corps stirred the blood and the Silent Drill team brought the crowd to utter silence.

There was something magical about watching men snap out precision moves, each in time with the other, with no sound but that of a rifle butt smacking into a gloved palm.

There was a sense of pride that rippled through the awestruck, motionless crowd.

A kind of pride no civilian could ever truly understand.

And as the Silent Drill team moved off the field, Tina Coretti Reilly, Emma Jacobsen Reilly and Terry Evans soon-to-be-Reilly, chatted in lawn chairs alongside their mother-in-law, Maggie Reilly.

Tina leaned out from beneath the rainbow striped umbrella, attached to her chair and held up a thermal jug of ice tea. "Anyone?"

"No, thanks, I'm good," Emma said, leaning forward, trying to strain her eyes to watch for a certain red convertible.

"Terry?" Tina asked.

"Yes, thanks." She took the plastic cup of tea and swallowed a sip before saying, "This is all so…"

"Amazing, isn't it?" Maggie said and gave Terry's hand a pat. "I always get teary at the official functions. And I'm so glad you're here with us for this."

"So am I," Terry said meaningfully, "and *this* I wouldn't have missed for anything."

"I hear that," Tina said on a laugh. "The Reilly Triplets in coconut bras?" she laughed again, clearly delighted at the mental image.

"Their friends will never let them forget it," Emma said smiling.

"And neither will we, dear," Maggie said and pulled a video camera out of the straw basket at her feet.

Terry laughed and looked at the older woman with the sparkling blue eyes so much like her sons. "You're going to *tape* them?"

"Of course I am," Maggie said, turning the camera on and winking at Terry. "Never pass up a chance for a little blackmail material on family."

"Ah, the Reillys," Tina said, leaning back in her chair and sticking her feet out to cross them at the ankle. "You gotta love us."

"We *are* fun," Emma admitted.

"Oh," Terry said, as she leaned back to sip her tea and enjoy the moment of solidarity, "I think I'm going to be very happy in this family."

"Look, girls," Maggie called out, excitement squeaking in her voice. "Here they come!"

A shining red Cadillac convertible slowly rolled along the main drive. Liam sat at the wheel, waving to the crowds, an enormous grin on his face.

Aidan, Brian and Connor, all sat on the trunk, their legs in the back seat. Each of them wore a coconut bra, a grass hula skirt and the grim expression of men trapped with no way out.

But as the crowd cheered, the Reilly triplets each lifted a hand in a wave—and met their humiliation like Marines.

* * * * *

THE SECRET DIARY

**A new drama unfolds for six
of the state's wealthiest bachelors.**

This newest installment continues with

LESS-THAN-INNOCENT INVITATION
by Shirley Rogers
(Silhouette Desire #1671)

Melissa Mason will do almost anything
to avoid talking to her former fiancé,
Logan Voss. Too bad his ranch is the
only place she can stay while in Royal.
What's worse, he seems determined
to renew their acquaintance…
in every way.

Available August 2005 at your favorite retail outlet.

If you enjoyed what you just read,
then we've got an offer you can't resist!

Take 2 bestselling love stories FREE!

Plus get a FREE surprise gift!

Clip this page and mail it to Silhouette Reader Service™

IN U.S.A.
3010 Walden Ave.
P.O. Box 1867
Buffalo, N.Y. 14240-1867

IN CANADA
P.O. Box 609
Fort Erie, Ontario
L2A 5X3

YES! Please send me 2 free Silhouette Desire® novels and my free surprise gift. After receiving them, if I don't wish to receive anymore, I can return the shipping statement marked cancel. If I don't cancel, I will receive 6 brand-new novels every month, before they're available in stores! In the U.S.A., bill me at the bargain price of $3.80 plus 25¢ shipping and handling per book and applicable sales tax, if any*. In Canada, bill me at the bargain price of $4.47 plus 25¢ shipping and handling per book and applicable taxes**. That's the complete price and a savings of at least 10% off the cover prices—what a great deal! I understand that accepting the 2 free books and gift places me under no obligation ever to buy any books. I can always return a shipment and cancel at any time. Even if I never buy another book from Silhouette, the 2 free books and gift are mine to keep forever.

225 SDN DZ9F
326 SDN DZ9G

Name	(PLEASE PRINT)	
Address	Apt.#	
City	State/Prov.	Zip/Postal Code

Not valid to current Silhouette Desire® subscribers.

Want to try two free books from another series?
Call 1-800-873-8635 or visit www.morefreebooks.com.

* Terms and prices subject to change without notice. Sales tax applicable in N.Y.
** Canadian residents will be charged applicable provincial taxes and GST.
All orders subject to approval. Offer limited to one per household.
® are registered trademarks owned and used by the trademark owner and or its licensee.

DES04R   ©2004 Harlequin Enterprises Limited

Available this August from
Silhouette Desire and *USA TODAY*
bestselling author

Jennifer Greene

HOT TO THE TOUCH
(Silhouette Desire #1670)

Locked in the darkness of his tortured soul and
body, Fox Lockwood has tried to retreat from
the world. Hired to help, massage therapist
Phoebe Schneider relies on her sense of touch
to bring Fox back. But will they be able to keep
their relationship strictly professional once their
connection turns unbelievably hot?

Available wherever Silhouette Books are sold.

COMING NEXT MONTH

#1669 MISTAKEN FOR A MISTRESS—Kristi Gold
Dynasties: The Ashtons
To solve his grandfather's murder, Ford Ashton concealed his true identity to seduce his grandfather's suspected mistress. But he soon discovered that Kerry Rourke was not all *she* appeared to be. Her offer to help him find the truth turned his mistrust to attraction. Yet even if they solved the case, could love survive with so much deception between them?

#1670 HOT TO THE TOUCH—Jennifer Greene
Fox Lockwood was suffering from a traumatic war experience no doctor could cure. Enter Phoebe Schneider—a masseuse specializing in soothing distraught infants. But Fox was fully grown, and though Phoebe desired to relieve his tension, dare she risk allowing their professional relationship to take a more personal turn?

#1671 LESS-THAN-INNOCENT INVITATION—Shirley Rogers
Texas Cattleman's Club: The Secret Diary
When Melissa Mason heard rancher Logan Voss proposed to her simply to secure his family inheritance, she ended their engagement and broke his heart. Ten years later, now an accomplished news reporter, Melissa had accepted an assignment that brought her back to Logan, forcing her to confront the real reason she left all they had behind.

#1672 ROCK ME ALL NIGHT—Katherine Garbera
King of Hearts
Dumped by her fiancé on New Year's Eve, late-night DJ Lauren Belchoir had plenty to vent to her listeners about romance. But when hip record producer Jack Montrose appeared, passion surged between them like high-voltage ariwaves. Would putting their hearts on the air determine if their fairy-tale romance was real, or just after-hours gossip?

#1673 SEDUCTION BY THE BOOK—Linda Conrad
The Gypsy Inheritance
Widower Nicholas Scoville had isolated himself on his Caribbean island—until beautiful Annie Riley arrived and refused to be ignored. One long night, one vivid storm and some mindless passion later…could what they found in each other's arms overcome Nick's painful past?

#1674 HER ROYAL BED—Laura Wright
She had been a princess only a month before yearning for her old life. So when Jane Hefner Al-Nayhal traveled to Texas to see her brother and a detour landed her in the arms of cowboy Bobby Callahan, she began thinking of taking a permanent vacation. But Bobby had planned to destroy her family. Was Jane's love strong enough to prevent disaster?

SDCNM0705